FEAR IS FOREVER

The Best Haunted Tales
of William P. Robertson

Published by **BookBaby**
www.bookbaby.com

CONTENTS

CREDITS

The stories listed below were first published in the following periodicals:
"The Spirit of Catherine," S*tride*, Cheshire, England; "Wide Spot in the Road," *Dominus*, Galati, Romania; "The Weight," *The Glasgow Magazine*, Glasgow, Scotland; "The Brown-Streaked Sidewalk," *A Time for Seasons and Holidays: A Creative with Words Celebration*, Carmel, CA; "When the Hunter Becomes the Hunted," *Tyro Magazine*, Sault Ste. Marie, Ontario, Canada; "The Price of a Pint," *Dark Starr*, Oceanside, CA; "Fetters and Chains," *The Black Abyss*, Philadelphia, PA; "The Crimson Tinge," *New Blood*, Ontario, CA; "The Goldenrod," *Prelude to Fantasy*, Minneapolis, MN; "The Eighth Wonder of the World," *The Bradford Era*, Bradford, PA. "The Spirit of Catherine" and "When the Hunter Becomes the Hunted" were also published in *The Pennsylvania Reader*, Wellsboro, PA. "Wide Spot in the Road" appeared in *Vega Magazine*, Bloomfield, NJ and on GW Thomas' *Flashshot* webzine, as well.

A special thanks goes out to David Cox for creating the cover. David may be contacted by email at dlcox1972@gmail.com. The publicity photo of Jim Morrison is courtesy of Elektra Records. All other photographs were taken by William P. Robertson or are from the Robertson family album.

THE SPIRIT OF CATHERINE

Excitement had me by the throat as I skidded along the mossy rocks bordering the headwaters of Five Mile Brook. Although I had left my car well before noon, I was now just nearing my destination. I had been so immersed in fishing for scrappy native brook trout that my exploration had taken far longer than I had anticipated. When I disassembled my fly rod and hightailed it upstream, the evening shadows had already begun creeping out from beneath the hemlocks.

The scabby cherry trees seemed blacker than I had ever before seen them. The wind also began acting like the plaything of a perverse magician. Although I was an experienced woodsman, I had difficulty pinpointing from which direction it came. Its howling seemed almost cyclonic in nature and was rising fast. In the fading light only my stubbornness pushed me onward. Finally, without warning, I stumbled through an orange screen of beech leaves and skidded to a halt on the shore of the blighted swamp I had been seeking.

Having no brothers or sisters to accompany me, I had hiked alone in the woods since I was twelve. Yet, even I couldn't help but shrink from the vile sea of muck and stagnant water that stretched before me in the twilight. Great bleached tree trunks reached finger-like from the fringes of this mire while ghostly beaver huts glowed in the mist now forming over the deeper pools. The distant chant of the whippoorwill made my face grow cold beneath my beard. If only I had asked a friend to come along. If only I had a friend to ask!

So this is where Catherine perished. No wonder the old Swedes wouldn't venture out here at night. According to legend, the girl had wandered off to pick Christmas ground pine and got caught in a driving blizzard. It wasn't until the following spring that her corpse was discovered by trappers near this very spot. Neighboring farmers swear that her cries for help can be heard echoing from these dark swamps even today. My grandmother said she was a winsome lass, wild as a colt and always out walking alone.

How strong the wind has grown. Yet, the mist, if anything, is swirling thicker. I must leave this blighted place before my imagination gets the better of me. I must turn and take one. . .step. .

.at. . .a. . .time. Just one step. Oh, God! I'm sinking. . .sinking!

Catherine? Is that you? My, your skin is so cold and smooth. You are a winsome lass. Now, we shall never again have to walk through this swamp alone. . .

WIDE SPOT IN THE ROAD

Gus Carlson reined his team of horses to a halt. Staring ahead down the desolate one-lane track, he could feel his scalp tingle as he contemplated the hemlocks that hemmed him in like the walls of a grave. Even on the brightest summer day it was an eerie road to travel, for little sunlight ever filtered into this tunnel through the trees. Today, Gus felt especially uneasy as he watched the thunderheads gather in the dark sky above and listened to the rising wind.

The horses seemed to share the farmer's uneasiness. Pulling a loaded buckboard up a five-mile grade should have tamed even the most spirited of animals. Yet, Gus suspected that the heavy lather on the black mare's flanks wasn't entirely due to physical exertion. The beast's nostrils were just too unnaturally flared as it stared wild-eyed into the gloomy wood. Even the gentle gray rubbed uneasily against the traces and had to be prodded forward with an unusual amount of coaxing.

When the animals finally plunged ahead, they broke into a full gallop. The buckboard jolted wildly down the slope with the farmer yanking the reins and crushing the brake for all he was worth. It wasn't until the frenzied beasts had bolted to the top of the next hillock that Gus managed to bring them under control.

Despite the frigid October wind, Gus discovered that he was soaked with sweat. Perspiration poured from under his hatband and dribbled onto his spectacles. With annoyance, he peeled off his glasses, mopped a coarse handkerchief across his forehead, and then proceeded to survey the distance with nearsighted eyes. From his hilltop vantage point, he could barely distinguish the blurry road ahead as it threaded its way across an infinite series of lower hillocks that rose like waves from the hemlock sea.

When Gus replaced his spectacles, he noticed an ant-like vehicle moving toward him up the road three knolls away. As he watched the other vehicle disappear behind the second hill, he wondered how they could ever pass on a wood-lined road barely wide enough for his own buckboard. The thought had little time to register before Gus saw the object of his concern miraculously appear atop the second knoll.

This time Gus had no trouble identifying the mysterious coach. It was somber, black, and unmistakably a hearse! It was drawn by six gigantic black draft horses that trotted along as if in a trance. How the brutes were able to pull that hearse three miles in three seconds was something Gus didn't care to ponder. Instead, he urged his own trembling team forward. Shortly after, to his surprise, he found a place to pull off and await the distant coach's arrival.

When the hearse disappeared behind the remaining hillock that separated them, Gus wondered why in ten years of traveling to market he had never before noticed this wide spot in the road. Nervously, he tugged at his beard and then at his watch chain. He produced an initialed timepiece that had been a gift from his eldest son, Herbert. The watch read one o'clock. It had to be later than that, he thought.

The farmer held the watch to his ear. It wasn't ticking. Had he forgotten to wind it that morning in his haste to get an early start? He twisted the winding knob and found it wouldn't move. While he replaced the broken timepiece in his pocket, a distant rumble of thunder made his horses fidget.

Gus waited for what seemed like an hour. When no vehicle appeared atop the distant knoll, he muttered, "Where could that hearse have gone? There's no side road it could have taken. And this one's not broad enough to turn around on."

The winds rose to gale force and snatched Gus' hat from his head. As he whirled around to save it, he gasped in surprise. There, disappearing over the horizon *behind* him was the somber, black coach for which he'd been waiting.

Suddenly, the black mare reared up on its hind legs, and the gray emitted an almost human shriek. Gus barely had time to grip the reins before his team was off and running. It never slowed until the dirt track blended into the brick highway leading into Gus' own gate.

When the buckboard swirled up the drive, Gus' wife appeared at the front door of their homestead. Her face was wan and etched with sorrow.

Visibly shaken, the farmer got down from the wagon. He walked absently toward his trembling Greta.

"Gus," she said blankly. "I have something to tell you."

"Yes."

"Our son, Herbert."

"Yes?"

"He fell down the well. . .Drowned. . ."

"Around one o'clock?"

"Dear Lord!" sobbed Greta, burying her head on Gus' shoulder. "How did you know? How *could* you know?"

THE WEIGHT

As Karl Johnson struggled with his burden, he felt his knees buckle beneath him. At this rate, he would never reach the barn that stood three hundred yards across the orchard. Reeling against the nearest apple tree, he righted himself to more evenly distribute the weight on his back.

"Vhy?" he wondered aloud. "Vhy did I come out in the woods so close to dark?"

Karl was a strapping youth. At seventeen, he was already well over six-foot tall. His two hundred pounds of bulky muscle helped him perform even the most rigorous of normal farming chores. From pitching hay, to guiding a plow, to digging postholes, to shearing sheep, he was the first of his family to finish his work and the last to complain of fatigue. But then, the weight with which he now found himself saddled, could hardly be characterized as "normal."

If only he had not been so skeptical of the old legends. Those, like everything else Swedish, he believed should be cast aside now that his family lived in America. "Vhy dvell on customs from the old country?" he had asked his father countless times. "If you loved the old ways so much, vhy did you put an entire ocean between you and them?"

Karl had another more personal reason for spurning his heritage. He was tired of being the brunt of the American boys' jokes. Often, his muscles had also come in handy when he ventured into town. At first, he had only used them when goaded into fighting by the taunt of "Dumb Swede!" That, however, was before he had thrashed every upstart farmhand within twenty miles and, in turn, had become the bully.

A faint tremor that most would have recognized as fear pulsed through the brawny lad as he again lurched toward the distant barn. He was soon forced to rest against every third tree he blundered upon in the growing gloom.

Sweat poured from the immigrant boy as he leaned panting against the rough bark of a hickory trunk. Closing his eyes, he was suddenly disturbed by a very real childhood memory. It was that of his grizzled Uncle Ole sitting hunched over in his favorite rocker croaking out tales of elfin lore. Face animated with firelight, the old man had delighted in frightening the children who gathered about the hearth to hear the stories he told every Midsummer Eve. The rest of the year he was seldom known to speak more than a few mumbled words. Too shriveled to work anymore, he spent most of his hours daydreaming or limping alone through the woods to gather herbs and mushrooms. These Ole used in medicines he concocted for all the old crones of the neighborhood.

By far, his uncle's favorite stories involved the trolls—those hirsute creatures reputed to haunt the dank woodlands surrounding the Johnson farm. Karl remembered how loudly he had laughed when Ole, in the midst of his narration, would twist up his bearded cheeks in impish imitation and leap at an unsuspecting child nestled at his feet. Then, the old man would describe in hideous detail how after sunset the Little People dropped from trees to steal a ride on a human's back. By the time Ole had explained the trolls' ultimate intent in doing so, all the children (but Karl) were crying in their mothers' aprons. These stories still would seem ludicrous if it had not been for the pig-like bristles scraping against the back of Karl's neck.

Karl reached the edge of the orchard just as the final glimmer of twilight was fading from the sky. Eyes blurring with fatigue, the Swede now viewed the barn as a mere shadow outlined against the horizon. With the building still a hundred yards away, he felt an overpowering urge to sink to the ground for a quick rest. Only the smell of bitterroot reminded him of the consequences.

With his endurance fading fast, Karl recognized the need for drastic action, and he became infuriated by the whole situation. After all, what had he to fear? Had his brawn ever failed him before in any wrestling bout? Certainly not! It had never mattered what type of death grip his opponent had used. Why should it now?

Karl reached one rope-like arm over his shoulder. Instead of throttling the unseen enemy as planned, he found his range of movement shackled by his huge expanding bicep. Howling in a blind animal frenzy, the immigrant whirled around and around like a bear swatting bees, clawing at the empty air. When he felt the weight grow tighter to him still, he wildly butted his back against the next gnarled tree he encountered in the dusk. Each time he rebounded, a shockwave exploded in his brain.

Finally, everything went blank, and Karl slumped to his knees. The next thing he knew, he was instinctively stumbling in a dead run toward the barn. The brief contact with the ground had proven true his Uncle Ole's elfin lore. No blackout could compare with the empty nothingness of one's soul being slowly sucked away.

Karl was now totally consumed by fear. Nor had he ever before felt so alone. It was as if he were rushing headlong down a subterranean tunnel to hell. He could no longer feel his legs, but he knew they were working when the deeper shadows of the barn loomed up to engulf him.

With the radar of a bat, Karl veered off at a right angle to the barn wall and followed it along until he distinguished the faint glow of lantern light leaking from the bottom of a side door. He lifted the latch and ducked his giant frame through the four-and-a-half foot opening that had been purposely built that height by his superstitious father. As he did so, he heard a thump behind him and whirled in time to see an impish figure leap up and flee into the gloom. All at once the weight was gone from Karl's back. If only it had left his heart, as well. The imp had had his Uncle Ole's face.

THE BRAKEMAN

Farley Stokes jerked awake when an urgent blast issued from the train whistle. "Cripes alfriday!" he muttered. "Must be nearin' the Kinzua Bridge. Can't go more 'n five mile an hour over that mother. Shouldn'ta dozed off. Shouldn'ta!"

The engineer's signal warned the brakeman to get busy. Immediately, Farley scrambled to his feet and rushed out the front door of the caboose. Leaping onto the ladder on the end of the freight car ahead, he scurried like a monkey to the roof. There, Stokes found a rusty brake wheel that he broke loose using a heavy club. With his heartbeat thudding in his ears, he reefed on the wheel until he heard a grating screech below.

"Got nine more cars ta brake, by gum, an' that'll do her!" shouted Stokes. "Yes, indeed!"

Farley rose and sprinted across the boxcar roof. He choked on black coal smoke spewing from the engine's smokestack and somehow kept his balance as the train rumbled over an uneven stretch of track that nearly pitched him off. He summarized the consequences of one slip, when he muttered, "Wouldn't be 'nough left o' me ta feed the buzzards if I fell 'neath the wheels. Careful, Farley, careful!"

Stokes was a thin, wiry young man in his late twenties, and it took all of his athleticism to leap to the next car. It was a three-foot jump, and he flailed his arms and legs while he flew through the air. Landing with a thump on the roof, he sprang into action.

As Stokes furiously cranked the brake wheel with his club, he saw Howard, the forward brakeman, climb from the coal tender and begin working his way toward him across the top of the cars. Howard was a gentle giant of a man with a full black beard and rippling biceps. He wore a sleeveless shirt to display his huge muscles in all but the coldest weather. He had needed every bit of that brawn the day Swede Andersen went berserk!

As Howard told it: "Swede got fired when he stormed inta the Mt. Jewett depot a week ago wieldin' a double-bladed ax. He was lookin' fer the engineer he found coupled to his wife. Caught 'im in the act of fornication, he did, but the fella run bare-ass out the door before he could cut it off. Swede showed how he'd castrate 'im, too, hackin' a model engine in half before I disarmed 'im. In the ensuin' ruckus, Swede pounded a squad o' coppers an' a half dozen railroaders. He brung two axes just in case, snatchin' up the second before skedaddlin'."

18

"An' now Swede Andersen's lookin' fer me," croaked Farley as he lurched toward the next boxcar. "Cripes alfriday! Of all gol dang people, why did I git hired ta replace *him*?"

By the time Farley and Howard met halfway across the car tops, the train had slowed to bridge speed. They acknowledged each other with pleased grins, and Howard blared, "You're really gettin' the hang o' this here job, ain't ya, Stokes? You're a lot better fella to work with 'n that maniac Andersen!"

"An' you're a great guy ta learn from! Put 'er there!"

After the brakemen exchanged fist bumps, two whistle blasts sent them scrambling to release the brakes they had recently applied. At five miles an hour, the cars rocked less, making their footing surer while they rushed to complete their task. But the slower speed also made it easier for hobos to steal a ride, and Farley nervously scanned the brush line on both sides of the tracks as he moved toward the rear end of the train. His club had come in handy in dealing with transients, too. But against a double-bladed ax?

Exhausted and drenched with sweat, Farley had just returned to the caboose when the train rattled onto a long steel viaduct spanning the Kinzua Valley below. This bridge was the highest of its kind, and locals dubbed it the "Eighth Wonder of the World." The center of the span was 300 feet tall. Farley NEVER looked down when he crossed it.

"An' from here Swede Andersen throwed his dead wife," said Stokes with a shudder. "Yep, he spread her stiff arms like wings an' launched her with the wind toward Kushequa. She didn't make much of an angel with her head split open an' the brains leakin' out. An' the fall done her no good, neither. Erased what was left of her prettiness."

Farley closed his eyes and didn't open them again until he heard the train clatter off the bridge. They were entering a vast moor overgrown with orange beech thickets and stands of cherry with black, scaly trunks. The bogs and undergrowth made this the perfect hideout for a fugitive, and on three consecutive trips there had been an incident.

It was now late evening. When the sun sank into the swampy expanse, shadows spread across the tracks, blurring the real and the unreal. It was difficult to see here even in the daytime, so the engineer kept the train's speed at ten miles per hour to make a quick stop possible.

As the train reached the first cut past the bridge, Farley swallowed hard. This is where last evening he had discerned the most hellish roar. "Loud as an elephant it was," mumbled Stokes, "but deep an' guttural. It were followed by bellows that bore right inta me. Yep. Swede Andersen has gone bughouse!"

Farley stared out the window at the encroaching gloom. Over the clack of the rails he heard a whoop and saw movement in the brush beside the tracks. Whatever it was was sprinting faster than the train and breaking off branches six feet in the air as it crashed along.

"Big gomer that S-S-Swede," stammered Farley, blanching with terror. "L-l-look at 'im run!"

Suddenly, Farley felt ever so alone. *Should go up ta the engine,* he thought. *Ain't safe here. But I'd git knocked off the car roofs sure as snot by them low-hangin' branches I hears smackin' the caboose. Calm down, Farley. Calm down. . .*

Before Stokes could decide what to do, something large slammed off the side of the caboose, rocking it on its wheels. Peering out the window, he saw a massive boulder bounce onto the bed of the tracks and roll into a ditch. Another boulder followed the first and cracked the wall next to Farley's head. As it caromed off into the twilight, he shrieked, "Judas priest! How strong do lunatics git?"

At that moment the train picked up speed as it clattered onto a straightaway. Heaving a sigh of relief, Farley snatched the railroad cap from his head and fanned his flushed face with it. He longed for a gulp of whiskey to wash the fear from his mouth. He settled for a long pull of water from his canteen. Half of it he spit out the window.

The train only chugged a short distance before the engineer madly applied his Eames vacuum brake. There was a man sprawled on the tracks ahead and no time to summon the brakemen to the cars. Somehow luck prevailed, and the engine skidded to a halt inches from the body.

While sparks still flew from the locked wheels, Howard leaped from the coal tender to investigate. "My God!" he gasped to the engineer. "You best git down here!"

The abrupt halt had more dire consequences for Farley. It was his duty to light a red lantern and walk up the tracks to display it eighty yards from the end of the caboose. It took him three tries to work up his courage before venturing into the dusk. Gooseflesh rose on his quaking legs as he paced off the distance.

"Swede Andersen be damned!" cussed Farley. "Gotta warn the next locomotive in case we's here a while. M-m-must stop it from r-r-rammin' us. . ."

What the lantern didn't stop was the mammoth biped that stomped from the undergrowth directly toward the light. Farley smelled it first as the odor of dung and death shot up his nostrils. The creature that erupted from the darkness added more crap to the mix. Instead of screaming, the brakeman filled his trousers when he saw it.

Impossibly tall, the beast was covered with black hair. Its head was rounded like a gorilla's with a pronounced brow and a low-set forehead. Its eyes were round, piercing orbs of almond light that fixed Farley like meat on a spit. It had an unusual method of distributing its weight. Raising its huge clawed hands, it strode with absolute menace toward the frozen brakeman.

Farley gripped his brake club with all his might, knowing it wasn't enough to keep Sasquatch from crushing his skull. He never learned it was Swede Andersen who was mutilated on the tracks ahead. His arms would be eaten, too, along with his heart and liver.

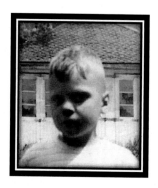

MRS. BABCOCK'S ABC'S

It was late afternoon, and pudgy Perry Black sat alone in his second grade classroom. Even the casual observer would have seen he was scared. His red freckles stood out like chicken pox on his pale cheeks, and his hands twisted nervously in his lap. His teacher sure was taking her time returning from the principal's office. Knowing her sadistic tendencies, the boy figured *that* was part of the punishment.

Perry stared at the clock above the door and saw it was 3:22. He heard the last of the buses rumble out of the parking lot. Once they were gone, an eerie silence crept over the schoolyard. Inside, the building was even quieter. The prisoner squirmed listening to the distant rattle of the furnace pipes below him.

Now, my parents gotta pick me up, an' school ain't the only place I'll be in trouble, Perry worried. *Our farm's far out in the country, and Pa sure hates quittin' his chores to drive way into town. This time I'm gonna get a whippin' for sure.*

Perry's nose wrinkled in disgust while he pondered the source of his trouble—Mrs. Babcock. "What a nasty, old witch she is, anyway!" he grumbled under his breath. "If she ain't rippin' on me with that sharp tongue of hers, she's rappin' my fingers with a ruler. Even worse, she gives me so much homework I can't play Peewee Baseball. I still don't see why Ma thinks 'rithmetic is more important than smackin' long home runs. There's no dang escape from Babcock's torture."

The boy also hated how dark his teacher kept the room. She never let in any sunshine. Last week she clawed him good when he tried to open the blinds and show her a rainbow he'd seen during recess. Now, the light was so dim, he could barely make out the print of the Dick and Jane book he was assigned to finish. He was behind a grade in reading as the hag was constantly reminding him.

There's no way to get back at old Babcock, either, the boy reflected. *She never sits down without checkin' her chair for tacks. An' crap! She actually **likes** the snakes an' toads I put in her desk. I'll bet she makes soup out of 'em. Yeah, and it only made her laugh the time I yanked out my loose tooth an' dribbled blood on her new pantsuit. I wiggled the tooth all day so I could pull it out when she bent over to get my math test after sixth period. Wow! Did she get excited seein' my blood. That was creepy!*

Today, in desperation for revenge, the boy had attempted to slip a rotten apple into Mrs. Babcock's lunch sack while she was in the hall

24

gossiping with another teacher. The apple was so decayed that even the pigs wouldn't eat it. If his classmates hadn't burst out laughing, he'd have gotten away with it, too.

"All the sixth graders say Mrs. Babcock's a ghoul," mumbled Perry. "That's why she always comes to school before daylight and goes home after dark. But who can believe them? Sixth graders will say anything to scare a little kid. They also told me the principal sleeps in a coffin down in the basement.

Perry looked in his desk and took a quick inventory of his cache of weapons. There were two spitball straws, a rubber band gun, and three bobby pin snappers. *These might keep away Dan the bully,* he thought, *but they sure won't protect me from that crone—Babcock.*

The boy continued to dawdle until the sound of hurried footsteps reverberated from the hall. By the time his teacher entered the room, Perry's nose was once again buried in his first grade reader. He had perfected his fake study techniques so he could even fool his mother. He felt he could carry this off long enough to be sent on his way home.

Mrs. Babcock glared balefully at her student. Seeing he was holding his book upside down, she screeched, "Dick and Jane would run much faster if they weren't standing on their heads!" To drive home her displeasure, she pinched Perry's fat cheek before returning to her desk.

Reddening, Perry flipped over his text and hid behind the cover. Even reading was better than looking at his teacher. Not only was she tall, gaunt, and ugly, but the lad hated how her bones showed through her transparent skin.

"Perry!"

The boy sat up with a start and found Mrs. Babcock scrutinizing him. It gave him the willies the way she kept staring at his fat arms. *Now, I know how the Thanksgiving turkey feels when Pa inspects its drumsticks before decidin' whether to cut off its head,* Perry reasoned.

"What's the matter with you, boy?" snarled the teacher. "You haven't turned a page in five minutes. Have you forgotten how to read, or are you hatching another of those schemes of yours?"

"I ain't doin' n-n-nothin', ma'am," stammered Perry.

"That's obvious," croaked the cadaverous woman slyly as she yanked open her desk drawer. "I think it's time we reviewed our ABC's."

"A-A-ABC's?" bleated the scared lad.

"Yes, my devious little fellow, *A* is for *apple.*"

Perry swallowed hard as he watched Mrs. Babcock produce the piece of decayed fruit that he had tried to slip into her lunch bag. She took a bite out of the rottenest spot and then sucked a worm from the core like it was a strand of succulent spaghetti. After licking the brown slime from her lips, she said, "And *B,* of course, is for *boy*—a plump, tender boy for supper!"

Perry leaped up screaming and bolted for the door only to find Principal Thomas blocking his exit. The towering man smiled broadly to reveal a mouth full of sharp, yellow fangs.

From behind Perry echoed Mrs. Babcock's screeching laughter. "And then there's *C,*" she cackled, rising menacingly from her desk. "I'll bet even you can guess what that stands for."

Perry glanced warily at his teacher and shook his head. "No." Then, he dodged back into the classroom just as the principal lunged to grab him.

"*Crimson* is the answer you're looking for," Mr. Thomas thundered, while he and Mrs. Babcock backed Perry into a corner. "Crimson is the color of blood—warm, tasty human blood."

RESCUE AT THE DEVIL'S DEN

"If someone would stop throwing gumdrops long enough to listen," barked tour guide Pitts, staring angrily at the smirking fat kid in the backseat of the bus, "I would like to tell you about the Valley of Death we are now entering."

"Yeah, throwin' stuff is rude, Stevie," said Gregory, elbowing the scrawny boy next to him in an effort to pass the blame. "Pay attention to the man. He knows everything about the Civil War. I'll bet he was at Fort Sumter when the first shot was fired."

Scoutmaster Morgan fixed Greg with a withering glare. Afterward, he growled, "You're not fooling anyone, Gregory Battles. I'll bet your granddad would be greatly disappointed in your behavior. Maybe I should call him when we get back to Wellsboro."

Greg glanced sheepishly at the furious scoutmaster and then muttered something behind his hand that made Stevie snicker. Only after Mr. Morgan stood and took a step toward them did the lads assume the proper decorum.

To avoid further conflict, Greg pretended to pay attention to the bearded Mr. Pitts when he gestured out the window and droned, "We are now on Crawford Avenue. To your left you will see a boulder-strewn hill called Little Round Top where some of the fiercest fighting took place here at Gettysburg. On Day Two of this epic battle, a determined group of Pennsylvania volunteers positioned on Little Round Top stopped an all-out Confederate assault meant to turn the Union's left flank. After repulsing the Rebels' charge, the troops of General Samuel Crawford counterattacked, drove the Confederates down the slope, and pushed them across the marshy valley bottom where you see Plum Run meandering along not far from this road. The fighting was grim and often involved bayonets and rifle butts when muskets misfired or couldn't be loaded fast enough. Some men's deaths were so violent and sudden that their ghosts were set loose to roam Gettysburg forever. Specters rose everywhere about this valley running red with soldiers' blood and are still seen today by those attuned to the supernatural."

As the scouts gawked out the windows to follow the guide's narration, Gregory pulled a thick rubber band from his pocket, stretched it to its full length, and snapped Stevie wickedly on the ear. The surprised boy's scream punctuated the historian's frightful tale of disembodied souls. His tears brought a shower of catcalls and taunts of "Do ghosts scare little Stevie?" Soon, chants of "P-o-o-r Stevie! P-o-o-r Stevie!" roared from every corner of the bus.

Red-faced, the tour guide howled for silence. It took the badgering of the scoutmaster and several adult chaperones before order was restored. Afterward, Mr. Pitts cleared his throat twice and yelped, "Off to the right, you will see the Rebel stronghold known as the Devil's Den. From this rock formation, Confederate snipers shot Union officers and artillerymen over a quarter of a mile away on the summit of Little Round Top."

"Yeah, right!" said Gregory while faking a cough. Then, he whispered to Stevie until a ripple of laughter replaced the glum boy's sullenness.

"What's so funny?" cried Mr. Morgan, leaping into the aisle. "I swear I'd like to throttle you, Steven Mack! What did Gregory say? Well?"

"T-t-that he could h-h-hit a Yank with his s-s-squirt gun from here, too. . ."

"Is that so, Gregory? Normally, we stop and allow our scouts to explore the snipers' positions at the Devil's Den, but your behavior has made that impossible. It's too bad your whole troop will have to miss seeing this amazing natural fort."

Again, all eyes fastened on Stevie Mack and Greg Battles. As the scouts screamed to vilify them, Mr. Morgan growled, "It looks like you boys don't want lunch, either. One more outburst, and I'll see that's arranged."

Wrapped in gloomy silence, the bus wound around a sharp curve encircling the jumble of gray boulders splotched with lichen. This now forbidden landmark of the Devil's Den made every lad itch to climb the erosion-smooth rocks and worm through the crevasses. Every patch of brush and pile of boulders that could have hidden a single Rebel sharpshooter looked inviting. Stevie and Greg stared longingly out the rear window until the rock formation disappeared from view.

"Cripe, if we hadn't watched that keen battle this morning, I'd be ready to go home," whispered the fat boy to his pal.

"Yeah, the reenactors were great! Too bad we couldn'ta talked to them Yanks an' Rebs an' looked at their guns an' stuff. Everything they had was true to history accordin' to Mr. Pitts."

"I wish that dang Pitts was history," snickered Gregory. "Then, we wouldn't have to listen to all his Little Round Top and Valley of Death crap. I already know everything he told us, anyhow."

"Sure ya do. . ."

After rolling past a display of cannon, the bus entered a dense wood. Here, it circled past several more monuments and then braked to a stop before an impressive statue of a Union soldier. The soldier struck a confident pose with his left arm held akimbo. Gripping a long musket in his right hand, he stared off into the distance as if he'd just whipped the whole Confederate Army by himself.

"What's that on the statue's hat?" asked Stevie.

"Looks like a hot dog in a bun to me," chuckled Greg. "I must be hungrier than I thought."

"No, Mr. Battles," corrected Scoutmaster Morgan. "If you bothered to read the inscription, you'd see it's a buck tail. It symbolizes the shooting ability of these men, who often survived by killing deer for food before the Civil War. The regiment wearing these tails on their kepi caps came from Northwestern Pennsylvania and is a

31

proud part of our state's heritage. That's why we stopped here to show you this monument. I myself had a Bucktail relative who was wounded here at Gettysburg."

"Yeah, the Bucktails were excellent marksmen," agreed the tour guide. "They usually served as skirmishers for the Union Army."

"What does that mean?" asked Stevie.

"It means they were the scouts who went out looking for the Rebels and often encountered the enemy first. They were like today's elite Army Rangers."

"The Bucktails must have been real tough then, huh?"

"That's right, Mr. Mack," replied the scoutmaster. "Why, at Harrisonburg they ran smack-dab into an entire Confederate brigade. Although outnumbered five to one, they killed General Turner Ashby and five hundred of his soldiers. It wasn't until half the Bucktails lay wounded on the ground that they were forced to retreat."

"Wow!"

"And at Antietam," continued Mr. Morgan, "they engaged the Rebels the evening before the main battle began. After being raked by wicked cannon fire, they chased the Southerners into the East Woods and had to fight there all night to hold the enemy at bay. The Bucktails further distinguished themselves at Fredericksburg. While the rest of the Union Army got whipped soundly by Robert E. Lee, the First Pennsylvania Rifles were the only Yankee troops to break through the Confederate lines stretched out on the high ground above the Rappahannock River."

"Who were the First Pennsylvania Rifles?" inquired a wide-eyed lad, tugging at the scoutmaster's elbow.

"I'm sorry. I didn't mean to confuse you. That's the other name the Bucktails went by, along with the Thirteenth Pennsylvania Reserves."

"But by the time they fought at Gettysburg, they had joined the Federal Army," reminded Mr. Pitts. "They were then known as the 42nd Pennsylvania Volunteers."

"Did the Bucktails find the Rebs first in this battle, too?" asked Stevie.

"No, they were stationed near Washington when Lee's army began its invasion of the North, so they had a long, hot march to get here. After a week's trek, the Bucktails still had to hike all night to arrive in time to join the battle on Day Two. Can you imagine marching ten miles in wool uniforms, lugging heavy rifles, blankets, and haversacks and then fighting the enemy? They didn't have much time to sleep, either!"

"Can't we eat now?" grumbled Gregory. "The only battle I want ta win is with my growlin' stomach."

"A-w-w-w-w! First, let's hear why they built this monument for the Bucktails," pleaded Stevie, remembering the smack his friend had given him on the ear. "You can wait a little longer, can't ya, Greg?"

"I'm glad that you're interested," replied the guide with a wide smile. "The 42nd Pennsylvania definitely deserved to be recognized for its role here. The regiment held the extreme left flank of the Union line on Little Round Top and helped drive the Rebels from the summit back across the

Valley of Death to the Devil's Den. It might have even chased the Rebs from there if darkness hadn't fallen. The regiment's colonel at one point was well in advance of the other charging Yanks, leading by his brave example—"

"Thank you, Mr. Pitts," interrupted the scoutmaster. "I hate to stop your fascinating tale, but I think we better have lunch before our own troops get too restless. This is also a good place for us to stretch our legs."

With an exuberant shout, the scouts leaped from their seats and pushed up the aisle, nearly trampling Mr. Morgan and the bearded historian in their stampede. The boys charged off the bus and romped about the Bucktail statue while the adults unloaded cardboard boxes stuffed with sandwiches, apples, bananas, cookies, and grapes. When the lads surged forward to be fed, a displeased chaperone observed wryly, "You'd think it was our boys who had marched all night to get to Gettysburg. They act like they haven't eaten since leaving Wellsboro yesterday morning."

"The way they're pushing, I'll bet they'd settle for slimy salt pork and weevily hardtack the Civil War soldiers ate," grunted Mr. Pitts.

"I'm just glad we're serving lemonade instead of Coca-Cola," replied Morgan, "or they'd want to reenact Pickett's Charge."

Just then, Gregory crowded up to the scoutmaster to get his lunch. "I'm sorry for throwin' stuff on the bus, sir," he mumbled. "I must have left my manners at home."

"Apology accepted, Mr. Battles. Now, move along. We have a schedule to keep."

Stevie Mack squirmed from the jostling mob next. His lunch box barely touched his hand when Gregory began herding him toward a small marker to the left of the Bucktail monument where no one else sat. The marker resembled a tombstone. It had a Bucktail cap and an epitaph carved on it. Greg scanned the inscription and then whispered to the boy he had corralled, "While the grownups are busy, why don't we sneak off to the Devil's Den an' eat?"

"But w-w-what if we get caught?" stammered Stevie.

"We'll never be missed if just the two of us go. Come on. It's not that far."

"I-I-I don't know. . ."

"Hey, you wanna see where the snipers hid out, don't ya?"

"I guess. . ."

"Then, let's go!"

"Are you sure we won't get in trouble?"

"Come on, you sissy! Nobody'll notice."

"But I don't wanna go where all those d-d-dead guys were."

"Then, you better not sit here either," said Gregory, "because a Bucktail officer bit the dust on this very spot."

Stevie leaped from the marker he was resting against, and Battles led him along the fringe of the crowd that nearly engulfed the bus. Next, the two boys nonchalantly wandered down the road, using the mob to shield their progress from the swamped adults. They pretended to be interested in a neighboring monument erected from three huge boulders for the 5th New Hampshire Regiment. When no one yelled after them, they disappeared behind the monument and lit out for the Devil's Den.

The boys kept to the brush until they could no longer hear the impatient voices of the famished scouts. Returning to the road, they walked briskly along munching on sandwiches between triumphant snorts of laughter. While they finished their lunches, Greg stopped to inspect a display of field cannon and a monument featuring a Union artilleryman holding a ramrod.

"Come on!" urged Stevie nervously. "Let's get goin'! It looks like it's gonna rain."

"Keep your shirt on," grunted the fat boy. "My granddad used to be a battlefield guide here until he had heart trouble. He taught me all about Civil War cannons an' stuff. He knows way more than old Pitts. I wanna have a good look at these Parrots. Or are they three inch ordnance guns? Let me see. . ."

Stevie Mack continued to badger his friend while Greg inspected the field pieces. Ignoring Stevie's pleas, Greg pretended to load one. It wasn't until Battles pulled an imaginary lanyard and fired his cannon that he finally took to his heels. Despite his size, the boy could really run, and Stevie had a hard time keeping up. He chugged along behind the heavy lad until they bolted around a corner and spied the jumble of rocks they'd seen from the bus window.

"Wow! Them boulders are really high," gasped Stevie, staring at the rocks towering above him. "An' look at how many hidin' places there are an' walls made outta stones. No wonder they call this place the Devil's Den."

"A sniper hid behind those walls," explained Gregory. "He called them his *home.* An' look! There's pit marks made by return fire. Do ya know what kind of guns the Rebs used to shoot Yankees on Little Round Top?"

"No."

"Target rifles that weighed over thirty pounds."

"Like your gut, ya mean?" razzed Stevie with a nervous laugh.

"An' they had long octagon barrels an' twenty power scopes. That's why those guns were so accurate."

"How do you know? You're just pullin' my leg, aren't ya?"

"No, I swear it's the truth. My granddad told me all about target rifles, too. I'm not really dumb. I just pretend to be. . .sometimes. Can you imagine how the kids would pick on me if I was fat *and* a smarty-pants?"

"We still have to visit the museum this afternoon. I'll bet we'll see a target rifle there. Maybe we outta get back now before we're left behind. An' look at that sky. It's gettin' b-b-blacker by the minute."

"No! No! Let's climb to the top of those rocks an' get a real view of Little Round Top. We could pretend we're snipers and pop a few Yanks."

"I wouldn't wanna do that. After hearin' what Mr. Morgan said about the Bucktails, I'd rather be one of them than a dang Reb. Let's leave. Please!"

"Hey, I came here to scale them rocks, and that's what I'm gonna do!"

"But what if we fall?"

"That ain't gonna happen. Are you a baby, or what?"

With a haughty shake of his head, Gregory started up a gentle incline that led to the top of the first set of boulders. When Stevie saw how easy the path was to climb, he clambered behind his friend and reached the summit without breaking a sweat.

"Wow! That sure was a long way them snipers had to shoot," croaked the smaller boy, staring at the rocky hill across the valley. "I think our guide said it was a quarter of a mile."

"That's why I'll bet the braver Rebs went out on the next point," said Battles, gesturing toward the rock ahead.

"But they'd have to jump across that c-c-crevice to get there. It has to be f-f-five feet wide!"

"Ahhh! Anyone can make it if he doesn't look down. The way you whine like a girl, I wonder why I hang out with ya. I think I'll start calling ya 'Stevena.'"

"Who are you callin' a girl? I can run an' jump better than most guys in my gym class. Coach Green even says so."

"Well, go ahead. Prove it!" dared Battles. "Jump over to that other point. It's flat as a tabletop. Even Stevena can't get hurt landin' there."

"Okay, I will!"

Stevie measured the jump across the wide crevice with his eyes. After brushing away some loose gravel that littered the ledge, he backed up to get a running start. With a determined cry, he shot forward and leaped with all his might toward the flat point ahead. He flew across the deep fissure and landed on his feet well beyond it. He put on the brakes and stumbled several feet farther before coming to a halt inches from the cliff at the end of the rock formation. Afterward, he spun around and stammered, "I-I-I did it, G-G-Greg. Now, it's your turn."

"Not before you leap back over here," replied Battles with a weak grin.

"Back?"

"Yeah, it's not smart for both of us to get trapped out there."

"Trapped?"

"I was just teasin'," confessed Gregory. "I didn't think you'd really jump."

Looking toward his friend, Stevie saw that the rock he was on was much lower than the one he had jumped from. In order to return to safety, he had to leap over the crevice and up to a two-foot higher ledge. His mouth flew open at the discovery, and his legs turned to water. With a deep groan, he melted to his knees and cried, "How am I gonna get offa here? How? How?"

"Don't ask me," replied Gregory, helplessly kneading his hands. "Maybe I ought ta get help."

"Hey, don't l-l-leave me!"

"But it's startin' to rain. You'll never get off those rocks once they're slippery."

"Slippery?"

"You heard me. I gotta go."

Before Mack could further persuade him, a rumble of thunder sent Battles scurrying for the path that led to safety down the back of the Devil's Den. He had no sooner disappeared from Stevie's view when a heavy downpour began to pound against the rocks. It was followed by flashes of lightning from across the Valley of Death. Remembering a page from the scout handbook, Stevie immediately flopped on his belly and flattened himself out.

The boy burst into tears as the cold rain pummeled him and a gusting wind whipped his drenched clothes. Shivering uncontrollably, he blubbered, "I gotta get off this point. I just gotta!"

Stevie continued to sob until he saw a tall figure appear on the ledge recently vacated by Battles. The man was dressed in a stained, tattered uniform of Yankee blue. He had a youthful face and kind, hazel eyes. His dark hair and goatee made his fair skin look even more pallid. Despite his youth, the soldier carried himself with an air of authority that caused Stevie to notice the colonel's eagles sewn on the shoulders of his uniform.

"It looks like you got yourself into a pickle, laddie," shouted the young officer. "Don't worry. I'm here to help."

"You a Bucktail reenactor?" cried the boy, seeing the white tail sewn on the colonel's kepi cap.

"Yes, I'm a Bucktail. Fred Taylor to be exact."

"I'm S-S-Stevie Mack. Everyone's gonna call me 'Stupid' when they f-f-find me."

"Don't run yourself down, laddie. You jumped out there on a dare, didn't you?"

"Yes, sir. How do you know?"

"I did plenty of foolish things myself for the same reason. I couldn't seem to help it. I was impetuous by nature. Like the time I gave myself up to the Rebs at Harrisonburg to tend the wounds of Colonel Kane. I was just a captain then and took some real kidding from the Bucktails after I got exchanged."

"Wow! You take your reenacting seriously. I watched your battle this morning, and did it look real with cannons blastin' an' the smoke rollin' an' the bayonets shinin' in the sun. All the hand-to-hand fightin' looked real, too. You must be really brave."

"And I'll bet you're a brave lad, too, Stevie. You're related to Samuel Mack, aren't you?"

"How do you know I have a great uncle Sammy?"

"I knew him back in '63, and you're his spittin' image when he was a might younger."

"And you say he was brave?" asked Stevie as the rain stopped and the sun burst through the clouds like a glowing ball of fire.

"Didn't you know he fought at Gettysburg? After we chased the Rebs into the woods over yonder, it was your uncle who went forward to scout out their position just before it got dark. After all the fighting we'd been through that day, he wanted to make sure the enemy didn't outflank the rest of us Bucktails and cut us to pieces."

"An' I look like him?"

"Yes, an uncanny likeness. Now, let's get you back to safety."

"Are you sure you're u-u-up to it?" stuttered Stevie, noticing the deep crimson stain on the breast of the other's coat. "Did you hurt yourself in t-t-today's reenactment?"

"Just a scratch, laddie."

"Okay. I guess I'm r-r-ready. . .If you are."

"Then, get up and walk to the far end of that point. It shouldn't be slippery now," said the colonel, pointing to the steam of evaporating moisture rising from the rocks in the sunshine.

Stevie wobbled to his feet and took one fearful step. When his canvas sneakers didn't slide, he took another and another until his confidence returned. With a weak grin, he walked as far as he dared toward the end of the point. After what seemed like an eternity, he turned to face the colonel, who continued to shout encouragement.

"All right, Private Mack. When I give you the command, run as fast as your legs will carry you. Remember. Jump high. Go!"

Stevie tore across the top of the point. He rushed though the rising steam until he was at the very brink of the crevice separating him from the beckoning officer. Then, he launched himself into the air and flew toward the other ledge. He hit the opposite rock with a terrific thud that knocked the air from his lungs. His toes churned in the loose gravel, and he clawed for a handhold on anything that would keep him from pitching backward into the yawning fissure he had cleared by only a couple of inches. He felt himself sliding backward into the abyss when a pale hand shot out and dragged him to safety.

For many minutes Stevie Mack lay shivering. Pain throbbed through his skinned knees, and his heart pounded from his brush with death. When he finally looked up to thank his rescuer, he found himself alone on the rocks.

Still trembling, the lad staggered to his feet and peered down the backside of the Devil's Den. Below him, he saw the tall colonel striding toward the path that led to the Bucktail Monument. Before Stevie could yell to him, the soldier vanished into the thick woods.

Blinking back tears, the boy tottered down the incline leading from the jumble of rocks. He hadn't gone far before he heard voices rushing toward him. The next minute, he found himself being mobbed by Gregory Battles, Mr. Morgan, and a dozen scouts.

"So ya saved yourself, did ya?" shouted Greg, slapping his friend wildly on the shoulder. "Ya saved yourself! Saved yourself!"

"I'm so glad you're okay!" yelped the scoutmaster with a relieved grin. "Why, you're soaking wet. That rain sure came down. Here! Throw this blanket around your shoulders before you catch a cold."

"D-d-did any of you see a Bucktail soldier?" asked Stevie through chattering teeth. "He-h-he was headed right toward you."

"We didn't see anyone," said Battles.

"But you musta passed him," insisted the lad. "I saw him come this way."

"Passed who?" asked Mr. Morgan, handing Stevie a thermos of lemonade.

"Colonel Taylor is who. H-h-he's the one who saved me."

"Colonel Fred Taylor?" gasped Gregory, his fat face turning suddenly white. "That can't be!"

"What do ya mean it c-c-can't?"

"We sat at *his* memorial before we sneaked off. Taylor was killed here in the woods on July 2, 1863. . ."

THE BROWN-STREAKED SIDEWALK

As the three boys squeezed through the crowd and out of the circus tent, their air of gaiety vanished. They had just spent two joy-filled hours giggling at clowns, ooing at trapeze performers, and clapping (between big bites of cotton candy) at the elephant act. Now, it was time for the long trek home across town *in the dark*.

Buster, the oldest, assumed command once they left behind the smoky brilliance of the Big Top. He was a hulking youth of thirteen, and a sadistic grin gleamed briefly on his rough features as he glanced back at his younger brother, Lenny. The little squirt had his ball cap crammed down over his forehead, concealing all but his very round eyes. He was dogging the heels of Buster's pal, Pete, and concentrated fully on tracing the larger boy's footsteps in the growing gloom.

Being a tag-along was about all that Lenny was good for. It seemed to Buster that he couldn't go anywhere without the little goof. And what made matters worse, their mother now expected him to drag Lenny along at night, too. Cripes! How were he and Pete going to meet girls if they had to wet-nurse the Squirt all the time? Well, maybe if everything went as planned on the way home. . .

To reach the distant lighted street, the boys had to cross a parking lot bordered by an abandoned baseball stadium. This ballpark once housed the Pony League team noted for developing such pitching stars as Elroy Face and Warren Spahn. No games had been played there in years, and now the peeling green walls and ramshackle clubhouse created a pool of midnight that even quickened policemen on their rounds. Needless to say, the boys avoided these deeper shadows as long as possible while circling the outer perimeter of the stadium.

Finally, they arrived at a murky tunnel that ran between the left field wall and a boundary fence. Here, Buster winked at Pete before deliberately quickening the pace. The moment they were totally immersed in darkness, they were off and sprinting for the safety of the streetlights, two hundred yards away.

It took Lenny awhile to realize he was alone in the dark. He fumbled blindly along, groping for Pete's shirt sleeves and whimpering softly to himself. Ten steps into the blackness, he finally dared peek out from under his ball cap.

A squeal pierced the night like a hatchet blade. Pete and Buster nodded meaningfully to one another and then glanced up from where they stood panting against a lamppost. It wasn't long before they perceived a dim shape streaking toward them around the corner of the ballpark.

Lenny emerged from the shadows hatless and out of breath. His face was pasty. His eyes glittered with fear. He gave no sign of recognition as he wheeled toward the older boys. If they hadn't grabbed him, he would have barreled into the path of an oncoming Chevy.

"What ails you?" howled Buster while restraining his brother. "Where's your cap?"

Lenny stared wildly at his captors and then nodded toward the eerie, dark tunnel.

"Hey, Squirt, you're not gonna leave it there. When we get home, Pa'll spank ya if ya do!"

"I d-d-don't care."

"Say what?" bullied Buster. "Why, I. . .I think you're chicken!"

The squirt flinched at the most dreaded word in a small fry's vocabulary, but he did not deny the accusation. Instead, he anchored himself to the lamppost in anticipation of his tormentors' next move.

"Don't tell us you're afraid of the dark," said Pete with a smirk. "Are you scared the boogeyman will get you?"

"Yeah, if you think you're big enough to hang out with us, you'd better get your butt back in there and get that hat!"

Except to tighten his grip on the lamppost, Lenny still did not move. Only after contemplating the murder in Buster's eye, did he squeak, "Okay. But you gotta go with me."

The older boys glanced warily into the pit of blackness bordering the stadium before echoing, "Go with you?"

"S-s-sure. . ."

"You gotta be kiddin'," muttered Pete.

"Ah, heck!" growled Buster, staring red-faced at his watch. "It's gettin' late. Forget the cap. Let's just get outta here."

When the boys dashed from the stadium parking lot, it was already well past eleven o'clock. Now, instead of taking the long, safe way home, they were forced to cut through the town refinery to make up for lost time. Straying from the well-lighted boulevard, they stumbled along a set of greasy railroad tracks between oil tanks two stories high. As they moved farther into the complex, towers loomed large, hissing steam and casting flickering flames across their path. With each new flare-up, Lenny sunk his claws into the back of his brother's jacket. He was too scared to notice how badly Pete trembled beside him.

Finally, even Buster could take it no more. Catching a glimpse of the streetlights at the far end of the refinery, he shook his brother loose and broke into a gallop with Pete close behind. By the time the bawling Lenny had caught up with them, Buster was as self-composed as ever and standing on East Main Street. "Well, Squirt," he growled, "what took you so long?"

Lenny dug his dirty knuckles into his eyes, precipitating a fresh flood of tears. "Why did you guys leave me back there?" he blubbered.

"Ah, shut up, you baby!" snarled Pete.

"If you're scared now," jeered Buster, "what are ya gonna do when we reach the witch house?"

"W-w-witch house?"

"You know. The one at the end of the block. Gee, I thought all big boys heard of that place."

The dwelling to which Buster referred had terrorized town kids for decades. It sat isolated on a bank overlooking East Main Street and was in a sorry state of repair. The porch was rotten, the shutters hung at crazy angles, and only the attic window was intact. It was there that "many a witch sighting" had been made, according to Pete.

"Yeah," added Buster, wishing to *enlighten* his brother. "Let me tell ya all about it."

And tell him about it, he did. As they scurried along the gloomy, tree-lined street, the bully conjured up tales of evil-eyed hags and disappearing neighbor boys that left Lenny a mess of twitching nerve ends. He was just finishing his ghastliest tale of all when they finally reached the overgrown lot occupied by the witch house.

With a wicked smile, Buster pointed up the hill and said, "And there, in that very window, they could see the old witch hacking up Jimmy Jones' body with a butcher knife *this* long!"

Buster made an exaggerated gesture and then glanced in the direction where he had pointed. When his eyes focused on a green face leering at him from the attic, he heard Pete gurgle a warning before tearing off down the street. The hairs on Buster's neck bristled, and he leaped straight in the air. The next instant, he was streaking in the same direction taken by his pal.

Halfway down the block Pete again came into sight, and Buster began to gain on him. As he was about to overtake him, he felt a rush of wind and looked up to see the little squirt, Lenny, zoom past and disappear around the next corner.

Blinking with astonishment, Buster muttered, "What the? How the?"

It was then that he noticed the brown streak on the sidewalk.

CAN YOU GIVE ME SANCTUARY?

Bobby Frederick's parents were at it again. He could hear them rumbling at each other through his locked bedroom door like two warring thunderheads. Lately, their squalling had become a nightly ritual. It seemed that the smallest thing would set them off. Planning next evening's dinner menu, rooting for different contestants on *The Price Is Right*, or bickering over the last beer in the fridge inevitably ended in an all-out screaming match.

"Oh, well," the boy sighed. "Still one place to go. Still one place to go."

Bobby leaned over, flicked on his lamp, and then crawled out of bed. Crossing the room, he stopped in front of an antique bookcase that sagged beneath the weight of an incredible rock 'n' roll album collection. These records provided the boy with much more than a pleasant pastime.

Over the years they had become his panacea and religion. Their power chords pumped up his confidence and, on nights like this, they shielded him from the horrible howl of his parents' altercations.

Of all the albums in Bobby's collection, it were those of the Doors that he held in special reverence. Unlike his friends, he had not bought the records to be cool. There was something about the group's eerie music that spoke of eternal sadness. What really hooked him, though, were Jim Morrison's tormented vocals. Whenever he heard the singer's anguish, he knew there was someone else who understood why he locked himself in his bedroom every night.

Bobby was introduced to the first Doors' LP at a stoner party. He had only gone to defy his father, not because he smoked weed. Even before one note blasted from the speakers, he was totally enthralled by the cover art—a photo of the musicians' blank, staring faces shrouded in darkness and mystery. By the time the radio staple, "Light My Fire," rumbled through the room, Bobby had already heard five incredible songs dripping with sex and dark imagery. It was "The End," though, that voiced the same growing alienation that was eating at the very core of his being. The song wove in and out of his head for eleven minutes and thirty-five seconds as Morrison unraveled a stark tale of Oedipal lust and mayhem. Its stream-of-consciousness mind trip was the most powerful experience of Frederick's young life.

After that, the release of each subsequent Doors' album became a major event to Bobby. He would haunt the local record shop for weeks until it finally arrived. Then, the record would remain on his turntable until he could growl out the lyrics to each song verbatim. It was after he had digested the Doors' second disc, *Strange Days*, that the boy let his hair grow down to his shoulders. He also bought his first pair of leather pants. Morrison's vision of life's unreality had won him a new disciple in spades.

But it was the *Waiting for the Sun* LP that cemented Bobby's Doors fixation. Its message of overt revolution and sensuality transformed him forever and spurred a dark quest for freedom. "Hello, I Love You" ignited an obsession with two hippie chicks that he shadowed every evening after school, aching for wild, debauched nights of sex and discovery that Morrison himself so reveled in. Then, "Yes, the River Knows" fueled a drinking problem Bobby only concealed by withdrawing further from his family. When his father started in on him about his appearance or strange behavior, the boy would scream out the words of "Five to One" and bolt from the dinner table. Morrison's politically charged lyrics no longer allowed Bobby to tolerate the older generation's power trip. It was after one such act of open rebellion that Frederick began wearing a single strand of Indian beads around his neck in emulation of his shaman—Jim.

Tonight, Bobby's sadness went much deeper than usual. He turned off his lamp and plugged in the black light that hung over his bed.

His wall-to-wall Doors posters sprang instantly to life. Bathed in their ghostly glow, he slid the *L.A. Woman* album from its protective sleeve. As he placed it on the turntable, he made sure not to smear greasy fingerprints on the grooved vinyl. To do so would have been like smudging a holy text.

Bobby cranked up the volume until the walls shook. He still couldn't believe that Morrison was gone! None of the facts of his death made any sense. How could the Word Man have had a heart attack while relaxing in the bathtub? And how could anyone be sure he was even in the coffin they buried at Pere La Chaise Cemetery? After all, only his wife, Pamela, and the mysterious doctor who signed Jim's death certificate had actually seen the body.

Bobby lay back on his bed and let the music wash over him. Neither the raucous rock of "The Changeling" nor the happy groove of "Love Her Madly" alleviated his pain. When he chanted along to the guttural blues of "Been Down So Long," he thought the words had never seemed so appropriate. Gripped by the powerful vibe, the boy leaped to his feet, his clenched fists upraised. Then, he snatched a pool cue from the corner and wielded it like a microphone stand as "L.A. Woman" exploded into his consciousness. He continued to writhe trance-like in perfect imitation of the Lizard King until the hot, hypnotic beat faded from the room.

Bobby turned the album over, flopped back on his bed, and closed his eyes. There was an angry rapping on his bedroom door, but the threat was thwarted by the booming vocals of "L'

America." The songs that followed allowed the boy to lapse into a dreamy reverie until the piano intro of "Riders on the Storm" rippled from the speakers. He did not open his eyes until Morrison's voice did not come bursting into the mix where it should have. It was as if someone had erased the vocal track from a song Frederick had heard hundreds of times before.

Bobby propped himself up on one elbow and stared through the eerie glow of his black light posters at the turntable. It was a Dual of the latest design and was equipped with a dust cover made of smoked plastic. Rising from the spinning disc beneath was a human head.

The face stopped rotating and became more distinct. It completely filled the space beneath the dust cover. The "Riders on the Storm" instrumental track continued to play as Bobby blinked in disbelief at the oh-too-familiar shock of brown hair and vacant, bulging eyes. The other features were as youthful and angelic as they had looked in 1967.

"Jim! Jim!" Bobbie gasped.

"It's hip here, man," replied the face after a moment.

"Where are you? You're supposed to be dead or. . .in Africa."

"On the other side of morning. . ."

"The. . .what?"

"Don't have to put up with a bunch of bullshit here, man. Don't have to stay loaded to make the scene. No hang-ups about sex, nakedness. . ."

"What about parents?"

"My old man, the admiral, would never make it here. Yours either. Dig?"

Suddenly, the pounding on the bedroom door grew louder and more insistent. Each rap was punctuated with the incoherent raging of Bobby's father. In a daze, the boy rose to his feet. Lurching toward his turntable, he muttered, "Jim. Jim! Can you give me sanctuary, Jim?"

"Sure, man. . .Just let me out. I'll help ya, man."

As Bobby approached his stereo, the music engulfed him. It took all of his strength to obey his shaman's command and lift the dust cover. Then, it was as if Morrison's voice echoed from the boy's own being. He never heard his father kick in the bedroom door. He stood transfixed, humming madly, watching the Elektra butterfly on the record label spin around and around. . .

NORTH HALL IS HAUNTED

"They don't call Mansfield a suitcase college for nothing," grumbled Susan, watching her roommate hurry to pack her clothes.

"What's a girl to do?" replied Sherry. "This campus is so dead on weekends that it's just not worth staying here. Why don't you split, too?"

"My parents won't allow it. They say they're paying good money for me to have 'the total college experience,' which doesn't include running back to *their* house all the time. My father even wants me to sign up for the summer semester."

"Then, why don't you visit your Aunt Celia? You're always talking about her. I remember how cool she was at orientation."

"My aunt's special all right. I wouldn't have survived adolescence if she hadn't helped me with my problems. But she already invited me for

Thanksgiving. I'd hate to impose on her now. She's so busy running her flower shop."

"Well, you could get yourself a boyfriend, Sooze. That'd keep you occupied."

"You know as well as I do that the boys on this campus are pigs. All they do is brag about their sexual adventures. You've heard them. They don't want a serious relationship with a girl. Jerks like that are only interested in one thing."

"But if you got interested in it, too," giggled Sherry, "you wouldn't have to worry about being bored. That's why they keep the TV lounge so dark, you know."

"I'd rather study until my eyeballs fall out than go to the Passion Pit with some hogman. I know what goes on in there."

"Then, what are you going to do for two whole days?"

"Work on my psych report, I guess. I'm assigned one every month. There sure won't be any noise to distract me with everyone else on our floor leaving."

"Aren't you scared to stay here by yourself after all the stories flying around this week about the ghost?"

"What stories?" asked Susan.

"Boy, you do study too much! The way I heard it, Debbie Weaver went up to practice the piano in the attic. As she climbed the stairs, she heard someone playing an old ragtime song."

"What's spooky about that?"

"When Debbie opened the attic door, the music just stopped. And there was no one sitting at the piano."

56

"Now, that is creepy!"

"What's creepy?" asked a surly girl after banging open Susan's door with an overnight bag. "Hurry up, Sherry. We don't want to miss our bus. My Delta Zeta sisters have already left for the terminal and will save us a good seat. I sure hope you pledge our sorority. We'd all love having you as a member."

"I'm almost finished, Barbara. I was just telling Susan about the North Hall ghost."

"The one Debbie heard?"

"You mean you know about the spook, too?" asked Susan with a look of trepidation.

"Sure!" replied Barbara, pulling a red beret over her silky hair. "You must be from Mars if you don't know about *her.*"

"Her?"

"Yeah, your dorm has been haunted since World War I. My sorority sister told me the story months ago. It seems this lovesick girl got really freaked out after her boyfriend was killed in the trenches of France. She started fooling around with a Ouija board and did all sorts of strange stuff trying desperately to contact him. Her parents, the housemother, and a psychiatrist all counseled her, but she would not listen. One night, after consulting the spirits, she ran screaming out into the hall and leaped down the stairwell. She fell six floors to the cafeteria where a security guard found her bloody, dead body. Every freshman class since then has seen her ghost roaming North Hall. And she lived right on this floor!"

"I guess I better keep my Ouija board in the closet," tittered Sherry. "I wouldn't want to rile up the spirit world."

"Or your spooked roomie, either," sneered Barbara, noting the hollow look in Susan's eyes.

"Hey, we gotta go, Sooze. See you Sunday night if you haven't shacked up with a cute boy by then."

"Or lapsed into a coma is more like it," mocked Barbara with obvious disdain.

"Get outta here!"

Waving goodbye, Sherry and Barbara shot out the door and merged with a constant stream of coeds making for the stairwell. The exodus continued for another hour until the sound of hurried footsteps, swishing skirts, and happy giggles were replaced by a deep, pervading silence.

To escape the ominous hush, Susan closed her door and turned on the radio. The only station that came in clearly was WNTE broadcast by the college. WNTE played a mix of Top 40 hits, and the girl plopped in front of the mirror to brush her hair and sing along to the Beach Boys. "We'll have fun, fun, fun!" she chirped in a breathy alto. "Yeah, right!"

Susan examined her oval face and full lips in the mirror. *Why couldn't I get a boyfriend?* she wondered. *I'm just as cute as Sherry. She's not kidding me. The "real" reason she goes home every weekend is to see that guy Steven she moans about in her sleep. I got nice, long hair that flips up on the end. And straight teeth, too. But*

why did I have to be born a dumb, old redhead?
Everyone knows we're all. . .so temperamental. . .

A sudden knock startled Susan from her reverie, and she leaped up to face the door. "W-w-who is it?" she stammered. "W-w-what do you want?"

"It's Mrs. Phillips. I need to talk to you."

Susan scurried to the door to admit a tall, brisk woman in her late 50's who served as housemother of North Hall. The lady stepped inside, and despite herself, checked the neatness of the room before saying, "Sherry Morgan just stopped by my office. Like any good resident assistant, she was worried about leaving you up here all alone. Are you going to be okay staying on this deserted floor by yourself? I have a spare bedroom in my suite downstairs if you'd like to room with me this weekend."

"Oh, Sherry shouldn't have bothered you. I'm fine," assured the redhead, imaging the ribbing she'd get from Barbara should she accept this offer. "I'm used to being alone. It's not a problem."

"Are you sure?" asked Mrs. Phillips, noting the strain in Susan's voice.

"Sure!"

"Oh, and I brought you a package."

"Thank you! Why, it's from Aunt Celia!"

"She sends these quite often, doesn't she?"

"Yes. She's my lifeline to the outside world."

"Then, it must be a care package, dear," replied the housemother with a comforting smile. "Would you like me to walk you down to dinner?"

"Okay. I could try to eat something."

"Be sure to lock your door!"

Susan turned off her radio. Then, she slipped on her tennis shoes and followed Mrs. Phillips down six flights of stairs to the basement cafeteria. There was no activity on any of the floors they passed on the way. The café was nearly deserted, as well, when the girl bid the housemother "good evening" and joined a short line of athletes who were also stuck on campus.

After filling up her tray, Susan sat by herself in a corner watching the football players wolf down steaming plates of spaghetti. Ever since she had arrived two months ago, the girl had practically lived on milk. Everything else she found undercooked or burnt to a crisp by the Mansfield food service. Not that her mom's meals were much better.

Susan glanced down at her tray and frowned in disbelief. "The cooks can even ruin Jello!" she muttered. "Yuck! They put onions in it. Those meatheads on the football team must be getting special food. How do they get their necks so thick? They can't even look sideways anymore! Not that they'd notice me, anyway."

Susan nibbled on a piece of Italian bread smeared with rancid butter that made her gag. With a disgusted frown, she picked up her fork and took a bite of salad tainted with hated radishes. When the spaghetti was too soggy to stomach, she leaped up and dumped the contents of her tray, dishes and all, into the trash bin.

In a huff, the girl stormed outside. She followed a sidewalk into a wooded park that stretched down the hill in front of her dorm. "My parents must really hate me to have talked me into coming here," she groaned, collapsing on a wooden bench. "So what if Father and Grandad are in the Mansfield Jock Hall of Fame? They were too busy scoring goals and kicking home runs to worry about being stuck in the Pennsylvania boondocks. The jocks aren't the only animals on this campus. We also have skunks, rabbits, and squirrels."

Susan burst into tears as she glanced at North Hall, the foreboding Gothic building that dominated the center of campus. "I hate my dorm," she bawled. "The towers are straight out of a Vincent Price movie. It's a wonder those windows don't have bars on them. And look at that ugly red brick. I swear this place would make a great sanitarium."

The girl covered her face with her hands and continued to sob until the long shadow cast by North Hall engulfed her. The sun was close to setting, and a few gray squirrels ran from the trees to dig for acorns before darkness fell. Their chattering roused Susan from her self-pity, and she became aware of a bitter cold that had invaded the late evening air. Shivering, she rose from the bench and trudged dejectedly up the hill toward the cafeteria door.

Back in her room, Susan resumed her disheartening conversation with herself. "I wish I was more like Sherry," she murmured. "She always knows the right thing to say. Everyone loves her to pieces even though she is a tough floor monitor. If she hadn't taken me in after the fight I had with my three roommates on second floor, I'd have quit college for sure. I just couldn't deal with sharing a room with that many girls after being an only child. I still can't believe Sherry let a loser like me stay in her R.A. suite."

Susan picked up her psychology text and leafed through it with disinterest. "It's a wonder my case history isn't written up in here," whimpered the coed. "The chapter title could read, 'The Invisible Girl.' That's me. It's like I never existed in high school. I had no dates, no club invitations, no one to notice.

"Even my parents didn't care if I ever left my room. They were too busy sleeping around to pay me much mind. Yeah, they fancied themselves real swingers. The way Father strutted about in his smoking jacket, you'd think he was Hugh Hefner. He didn't fool me any. Even a big executive like him could have had *that* many secretaries. And Mother was just as bad. Every Saturday night she left the house dressed like Zsa Zsa Gabor. When she finally did stagger home, she reeked of alcohol and strange men's cologne. Eeewww!

"And now that backstabbing Barbara wants to steal my only friend at Mansfield. I hate that snob. All she talks about is being a Delta Zeta. If she gets Sherry to join her little clique, I might as well *be* the North Hall ghost."

The girl slammed down her book and stared bitterly out the dorm window. The lights of the other dormitories glowed eerily through a dense fog that wrapped itself around the hillside campus. Braying laughter floated from the sidewalk below as a few nerds spilled from the closing library across the lane. "I'm so pathetic, I don't even fit in with those kids," sighed Susan. "I guess I'll go to bed. . ."

The redhead had just changed into her pajamas when she heard footsteps tramp deliberately up the stairwell and move to the far end of the hall. *That, thought the coed, must be one-armed Lefty, the dumb, old security guard, making his rounds. Like he could do anything if there was trouble.*

Susan listened intently as the visitor halted before a distant door and knocked twice. After unlocking and opening the door, he closed it again and moved on to the next room. Methodically, the doors opened and closed all down the hall until the footsteps were even with her chamber. Instead of the expected knock, the caller moved past to check the rest of the vacant sixth floor.

Must have seen the light shining under my door, reasoned Susan after the visitor strode by. *Maybe I'd better see who's out there. . .*

Working up her courage, the girl slipped on a pink bathrobe and a pair of bunny slippers. Then, she crept toward the door and grabbed the knob. The footsteps continued to grow fainter as she fumbled with the lock. By the time she peeped into the hall, the intruder had moved even with the stairwell.

Instead of old Lefty, there floated a misty figure in a baggy-sleeved dress. Her abundant hair was straight on top and curly down the back of her neck. She wore high-topped shoes and

63

dark stockings. Turning, she fixed Susan with a peaceful, dreamy smile. She opened her arms and beckoned with both hands before slowly fading from view.

With a gasp, Susan slammed her door and fought to lock it behind her. "A lot of good this will do," she croaked, "when the ghost has the floor key! Why didn't I accept Mrs. Phillips' offer? Damn my pride, anyway. I get that from Father, the pig."

The girl nervously brushed a stray strand of hair away from her face and then scrambled to turn on her study light. For good measure, she snapped on her roommate's lamp, too. Snatching her Bible from a shelf, Susan withdrew a crucifix Aunt Celia had given her as a confirmation gift and placed it in the breast pocket of her bathrobe. Finally, she collapsed on the bed to think things through.

"It figures I'd be the one that ghost appears to," ranted the coed. "Scary old Susan, spirit's friend. Too spooky for this world. Too weird to fit in. Thank God for the time I spent with Aunt Celia. She's the only loving person in my whole damn family. Why, I better open that package she sent me. Oh, look! She remembered how much I love chocolate chip cookies. Awww! A photo of her and me at the Thousand Islands, New York. We had such fun on that vacation. We shopped, swam, and took the boat tour. Why couldn't Celia have been my mother? She has respect for my feelings. *She* wouldn't have sent me to this spooky, old college."

Bursting into tears, Susan buried her head in her pillow. After she had cried herself out, she sat up and blew her nose.

"M-m-maybe I should see what the ghost wanted," mumbled the girl. "Didn't prissy Barbara say a Ouija board lets you communicate with the spirit world? Duh! I should know that. I just wrote a paper for psych class on Ouija boards. I even examined the one Sherry has in her closet while I was doing my research. There. I see it."

Susan crossed the floor and snatched the Ouija board from the top shelf of her roommate's meticulously organized wardrobe. With trembling hands, she pulled it out of the box and laid it on her desk. The board had a smiling sun painted in the top left corner with the word "Yes" next to it. In the top right corner was a frowning moon with "No" beside it.

The sun represents the God of the Spirit World, remembered Susan from her report. *The quarter phase moon stands for the Goddess of the Spirit World.*

Below the two images was the word "OUIJA" printed in bold letters and centered on the board. Under that, all the letters of the alphabet were stretched out in two rows from A to Z. A row of numbers from 1 to 0 came next. At the very bottom, Susan found the words "GOOD BYE."

My professor warned against using the board when I chose this topic, reflected the girl, tugging tentatively on her long hair. *I even listened to him. But that was. . .before. Even if spirit channeling is a dangerous business, I just gotta try to reach. . .that ghost. She seemed so happy. Something I want to be. Maybe. . .she. . .can help me. She couldn't be an evil presence, the way she was smiling. . .*

Susan picked up the wooden planchette and laid it on the board. The planchette was heart-shaped and had three felt-tipped legs that facilitated its movement. In the center was a plastic window to peer through.

Susan placed her right hand on the planchette. As she deliberately began circling the board with it, she asked politely, "Did I see the North Hall ghost?"

Susan pressed a little harder on the Message Indicator. She moved it faster. Suddenly, the lights began to flicker. A hair brush floated from the girl's dresser and hovered in the air. The girl screamed and let go of the planchette. Her hand no sooner sprang from the heart-shaped object when it moved on its own and spelled out the letters YES.

"W-w-why did you visit me?" stuttered Susan as the brush flew into her hand.

I FELT YOUR PAIN, answered the planchette.

As Susan read the message, the bulb in her roommate's study lamp flashed wickedly and exploded. Then, her psychology text lifted from the desk and began circling her head. Its movement had a hypnotic effect on her, and she asked numbly, "What should I do?"

The textbook dropped into Susan's lap and flew open to the chapter dealing with suicide.

Afterward, the planchette moved slowly and deliberately to spell JUMP.

A smile played across Susan's lips. She rose from the bed. Walking mechanically to the door, she turned the lock. The door creaked open of its own accord. She stepped into the hall. There, a sudden gust of cold wind mussed her hair and numbed her paling cheeks. She strode transfixed toward a wispy figure standing atop the stairwell railing. The figure smiled invitingly and held out her arms in a gesture of love.

Just before Susan reached the beckoning spirit, a second blast of wind blew her hair across her eyes. When she reached to push aside her bangs, her hand brushed across the crucifix in her breast pocket. The holy cross was warm to her touch, and she felt her heartbeat pulsing through it. Images of dear Aunt Celia popped suddenly into her brain with sun-filled afternoons and tall glasses of delicious lemonade.

With a shake of her head, Susan cleared the strands of hair blocking her vision. As she withdrew the crucifix and held it in front of her, she saw the ghost's sweet smile twist into a malicious leer. An expression of self-loathing and total despair revealed the fate that doomed its soul in 1917.

"The damned aren't happy!" cried Susan. "In the name of Jesus Christ, depart from me!"

With a fearful gasp, the ghost recoiled at the holy name. Before Susan could say "Jesus Christ" again, it lunged forward to snare the coed in its lethal arms. Susan dodged and bolted for the stairwell. In the next instant she was sprinting toward the fifth floor. No lights came on there in response to her cries for help, so she scrambled down, down, down into the bowels of North Hall. Blindly she ran with a cold wind shrieking at her heels, trying to capsize her. Only her instincts and awakened will allowed her to keep her balance as the wind buffeted her from behind.

Susan descended to the cafeteria just as her churning legs turned to rubber. She no sooner stumbled into the murky room when a hellish, disappointed wail filled the stairwell behind her. The cold, pursuing wind stopped suddenly and then sucked upward floor by floor until it vanished in the direction of the attic.

With the last of her strength, Susan crossed the cafeteria, pushed through the hallway doors, and staggered past the vacant TV lounge to Mrs. Phillips' suite. Fighting back the blackness closing around her, she rapped desperately on the smiley face taped to the housemother's door.

The terrified girl tottered on the threshold until a very sleepy Mrs. Phillips answered her flurry of knocks. "I couldn't jump! Couldn't jump!" babbled the coed, collapsing into the housemother's arms. "Help me. Please! Help me live. I want so much to. . .live. To thank Aunt Celia for her. . .love. . ."

THE LATE MR. WILSON

Ask any of my frat brothers. I've never exactly had a reputation for forethought. As a matter of fact, I always rolled out of bed five minutes before my eleven o'clock class and stumbled past the professor still half asleep with the pajama sleeves sticking out of my coat. That inclination also helps explain why I waited until two weeks before the start of the fall semester to enroll in graduate school at Mansfield State College in rural Pennsylvania where I had just spent four years earning my B.S. degree.

By then, naturally, all the decent housing in that small college town was taken. When I discovered that even the dormitories were full, I thought I might end up living out of my car. Just as the situation looked hopeless, I ran into one of my aforementioned brothers, who suggested that I visit a boarding house run by a Mrs. Wilson.

Following my friend's advice, I drove up a tree-lined avenue and parked my Ford Maverick in front of a huge, old clapboard mansion. When I rang the doorbell, I was smiling like I expected my fairy godmother to answer the signal. Instead, a ghastly pale woman in her late eighties whirred to the door in an electric wheelchair and regarded me with one bright, blue eye. A patch covered her other eye, and her hair was tucked up under a black net. Some of the luster went out of my smile when I regarded her bent figure, but somehow I still managed to inquire, "Is this the Wilson residence?"

"Yes, I'm Mrs. Wilson," replied the woman in a soft, steady voice that belied her infirmity. "May I help you?"

"I sure hope so. My friend, Tom Peters, told me that you rent out rooms, and um—"

"Oh, yes, I remember Tom," the old woman interrupted. "He lived with me two summers ago. He wore wire-rimmed glasses and studied day and night. Tommy was such a nice boy."

"Well, um, Tom, er, said that maybe you could help me. . ." And before I knew it, I was spilling out my problems to a perfect stranger who sat sizing me up with her one twinkling eye.

Even before I had finished, Mrs. Wilson was backing up her wheelchair and inviting me to "come sit in the parlor." Besides the immensity of the room, one of the first things I noticed was an oil painting that the lady admired periodically as she listened to me rattle on. It depicted a handsome young man in his late twenties. Characteristic of the Jazz Age, his hair was parted in the middle. The portrait had apparently been painted in this very room, for the mantle over which it now hung formed the backdrop for the gentleman's thin build.

"That's a real neat picture," I said as I plopped onto an overstuffed sofa opposite my hostess.

"I'm glad you like it," said Mrs. Wilson, obviously pleased. "That was my dear departed husband, Frederick. It was painted during the first year of our marriage by an art professor friend of ours. It has brought me many fond memories over the years. But then again, I suppose you haven't come here to listen to an old woman talk of such things."

"No, that's okay."

"Now. Now. I know in how much of a hurry you young people are these days, so I must confess that ordinarily I couldn't help you. . ."

I felt my heart sink as Mrs. Wilson paused to catch her breath. She must have noted my crestfallen expression, for there was a hint of kindness in her voice when she continued. "Keep your chin up, son. I only said that *ordinarily* I couldn't help. You see, all three of my available rooms are spoken for by nice boys who lived here last year. However, because you are a friend of Tommy Peters, and a graduate student to boot, I could let you have my spare room upstairs if you could rustle up a bed and dresser somewhere. Why don't you go up and have a look?"

After receiving instructions from Mrs. Wilson, I charged up the steps to the second floor landing. Directly in front and to the right of me were doorways that opened into two bedrooms. To the left was a long, narrow hall. I turned and strode twenty paces down this corridor until I came to the spare room to the left. Before

71

entering, I noticed a bathroom and a third bedroom farther down.

The spare room was cluttered with Christmas ornaments, tattered furniture, and boxes of old books. Other than that, I really liked what I found. Not only was it twice as large as my bedroom at home, but it also had a large walk-in closet that contained a stairway leading to the attic. It was even on the sunny side of the house and had two windows facing the college. Despite the giant weeping willow that towered just outside, I imagined there would be a nice view of the campus lights at night.

When I rushed downstairs to tell the dear lady how much I loved the room, her only comment was, "I know the late Mr. Wilson would be pleased to have you as a guest in our home." Then, she invited me to stay for tea and plied me with homemade cookies until I thought I would burst. As it turned out, the ten dollars a week I was to pay for rent would hardly have covered all the goodies she would make for her other boys and me.

So began one of happiest chapters of my college career, or so I thought at the time. After all, what could be nicer than having a third grandmother for a landlady? Come to think of it, Mrs. Wilson was even more understanding than either of my real grandmas. She never got angry when I tracked a little mud into her living room, and she always had an encouraging word for me when I'd stumble into the house after eight hours of research in the library. Even more unbelievable, she let me skin squirrels in her kitchen during hunting season no matter how big a mess I made. Man, what a wife she must have been!

Another swell aspect of living with Mrs. Wilson was the considerate group of guys she had boarding with her. All of them were honor students who spent most of their time studying or sleeping. It was great not having some jerk crank up his Alice Cooper records at three a.m. like in the dormitories. It also worked to my advantage that the other boarders went home every weekend. With a complete catalog of Henry James and William Faulkner novels to read, it was nice that the house got even quieter on Saturday and Sunday. Unfortunately, three months into the semester, it grew stiller than even I could have wanted. It was then, just before Thanksgiving, that the doctors discovered Mrs. Wilson had cancer and sent her to the hospital for radiation treatments.

About a week after our landlady was wheeled out the front door and loaded into an ambulance, I awoke chilled to the bone. For no apparent reason, Mrs. Wilson's new furnace died in the middle of the night. I tossed on my pants, winter coat, and a thick pair of wool socks and scooted for the bathroom. When I peered into the sink and noted all the soap scum and hair that coated its top and sides, I was sorry that I had remembered to brush my teeth that morning. Obviously, Mrs. Wilson's daughter-in-law had been spending so much time at the hospital that she hadn't done our scheduled housecleaning.

Without removing my toothbrush from the rack, I went downstairs and found one of the other boarders smoking on the sofa. His hands shook as, between puffs of his cigarette, he attempted to snip his toenails with a giant pair of scissors he had borrowed from Mrs. Wilson's sewing basket. I might have thought he was shaking from the cold if I hadn't noticed the pasty color of his face.

"Gee, Chuck," I needled as I sat on the coach beside him, "you look like you either chugged a case of green beer or just saw a ghost."

Chuck nodded toward the portrait over the mantle and then whispered, "Would you believe?"

"Would I believe what?"

"I know this is going to sound crazy, but something really weird happened. Did you hear any strange noises around two a.m.?"

"Heck no! Unless it was the chattering of my teeth. Man, I almost froze to death last night."

"Me, too. I even went down in the basement and tried for an hour to relight the damn furnace. *He* must have killed it before freaking me out later on."

"What was it you heard, Chuck?"

"It wasn't so much *what* as *who*."

I glanced sharply at my buddy and found him staring once more at Mr. Wilson's portrait. Chuck's face was etched with worry, and his usually piercing eyes were dull from lack of sleep.

"What do you mean by that?" I asked. "How could anybody get in here and mess with our furnace when we lock the doors every night before bedtime? You did remember to lock the doors?"

"There isn't a lock built that would stop this guy."

"Come on, Chuck. Will you stop talking in riddles?"

"Okay. Okay," replied my pal, lighting another cigarette. "Let me finish my story and then see what *you* make of it."

"Go on. Please!"

"Well, the whole thing started a few nights after Mrs. Wilson was taken to the hospital. A couple times earlier this week I was awakened in the middle of the night when I dreamed I heard someone call my name. I was a little spooked each time it happened but always managed to fall back asleep."

"Why didn't you say something before, Chuck?"

"I figured it was just my imagination playing tricks on me with the stress of finishing my term papers and everything. It wasn't until last night—"

Chuck's voice broke off, and the cigarette shook so violently in his hand that he crushed it out in an ashtray. Finally, he said, "Last night, as usual, I listened to the Knicks game on the radio. I apparently dozed off sometime in the second half. The next thing I knew, the station was signing off the air, and there was this voice right next to my ear whispering, 'Chuck. Chuck.' I might have thought it was another dream if the light hadn't been on when I opened my eyes. . ."

"What did you see?"

Instead of replying, my friend pointed meaningfully to the portrait of the late Mr. Wilson.

"Yeah, but h-h-he's dead," I stammered as the hairs bristled on the back of my neck.

Chuck smiled weakly before adding, "Maybe you'd better tell *him* that."

"But what *exactly* did you see?"

"He was only there for a minute. . .Uh, I mean visible. His face and suit like in the picture, only misty. I blinked, and he was gone."

"Holy smokes!" I exclaimed. "To get a ghost for a roommate is the last thing I need with finals coming up. Now, what are we going to do?"

Before Chuck could reply, a knock resounded through the house that made me leap straight in the air. With a stiff smile, Chuck rose quite calmly and went to the front door to answer it. After a moment he returned with a thin coed whose appearance did nothing to allay my own fears. If anything, I became more agitated upon noting her hawk-like face, hoop earrings, and dark, kerchief-wrapped hair.

"Bill, I'd like you to meet Janine."

As I nodded curtly to our guest, my friend added, "She's a psychology major and an expert on the supernatural. I've invited her down to help us solve the mystery I've been telling you about."

Chuck escorted Janine to the sofa and then disappeared into the kitchen. He returned with a tray containing a coffee pot, three cups, milk, and sugar. The girl, meanwhile, was studying the portrait hanging over the mantle. "Who is he?" she asked at last.

"That was Mrs. Wilson's husband," Chuck replied as he poured us each a cup of coffee. Then, he proceeded to recount to our guest the details of his encounter with that very gentleman.

The further my friend got into his tale, the more the coffee cup shook on his knee. Finally, Janine took it from his hand and set it on an end table. Afterward, she asked, "When and how did Mr. Wilson die?"

"According to the story I heard," whispered Chuck, "he passed away about ten years ago. He was chopping wood in the backyard and had a stroke. The strange part of it was, he never cried out for help, or anything. He just staggered back into the kitchen, where Mrs. Wilson was making apple sauce, and crumpled dead at her feet."

"He must have loved his wife very much," said Janine thoughtfully. "Did you notice any other disturbances prior to the ones you've been telling me about, Chuck?"

"No, in the three years I've lived here, this is the first time anything like this has happened."

"Yeah, it's funny how as soon as Mrs. Wilson left, things started going to pot around here," I added. "Even the furnace quit—"

"That's it!" shouted Janine.

"That's what?" I asked nervously.

"The reason for Mr. Wilson's sudden appearance."

"What do you mean?" blurted Chuck.

"Well, look. It's simple. Spirits seldom appear unless they're troubled by something. Just add up the facts."

"What facts?"

"Mr. Wilson dies ten years ago. Mrs. Wilson stays on here in the house. Suddenly, Mrs. Wilson is gone. She hasn't passed beyond the veil to join her husband in the hereafter, but she's not living here, either. This disturbs Mr. Wilson because he loves his wife so much. When she doesn't return after several days, he seeks information. That's why he calls out to you, Chuck."

"But why does he pick on me, Janine?"

"Probably because you've been here the longest, and he trusts you."

"Great! How can we get him to go away?"

"Well, I doubt if he will until his wife comes home."

"Even if I tell him where she went?"

"I don't think that would help. And besides killing your heat, who knows what other means he might use to show his displeasure over his wife's absence!"

"Other means?" I echoed. "Say, what makes you such an expert on ghosts, anyway?"

"My mother taught me. She's a psychic."

"Oh. . ."

"I-I-I'm sure glad it's Friday," sputtered Chuck. "At least I won't be here this weekend for Mr. Wilson to grill."

"But what about me?" I croaked. "I'm going to be all alone. And with no heat."

"Why don't you go home, too?"

"You know I can't leave, Chuck. I'm out of gas money again, and besides, I've got too much library research to do."

"Then, stay in your room at night," advised Janine. "Just stay in your room!"

That evening, as always, I went straight to the library after supper. Unfortunately, I found my annotated bibliography project a bit trivial compared with surviving the weekend *alone* at Mrs. Wilson's. Finally, around seven o'clock, I gave up researching altogether. I returned to the house before it got *too* dark.

As I hustled up Mrs. Wilson's front walk, a brisk wind whipped the trees lining the avenue. It was getting colder by the minute, and thick snow clouds powwowed above the roof of the house. My teeth chattered with more than the cold, however, when I finished fumbling with my key and worked the lock. With a shudder, I stepped inside. While I flipped on the living room light, the wind slammed shut the door violently behind me. I yelped with fear and about jumped out of my shoes!

Averting my eyes from the portrait above the mantle, I dashed to the fireplace and snatched up a poker. Brandishing it before me, I checked the kitchen, Mrs. Wilson's bedroom, and the first floor bath. After snapping on every light I encountered, I fled up the stairs and locked myself in my room. Naturally, I gave Chuck's bedroom a wide berth as I scurried past.

Even then I didn't feel safe. As I hung my coat in the closet, I remembered the stairway that led from it into the attic. Quickly, I slammed the closet door and shoved my dresser against it. Then, I closed the window blinds and turned on the stereo to muffle the howling wind. Without undressing, I crawled into bed still tightly clutching the poker. Naturally, I pulled the covers over my head.

So it was that I must have fallen asleep, for I never heard my favorite song on Santana's *Abraxas* album before the stereo clicked off. The next thing I clearly recall was jerking awake in a morgue-like silence that was broken periodically by a faint clumping on the front stairs. In a panic, I fumbled for the poker, rose noiselessly from bed, and pressed my ear against the hall door. Finally, I heard the muted sound of footsteps disappearing into one of the front bedrooms.

At first, I was too scared to do much more than keep my knees from banging together. It wasn't until the scraping of dresser drawers reached my ears that I remembered Janine's warning about a spirit's "other means" of expressing displeasure. Spurred by that thought, I unlocked my door and very cautiously opened it until I could peer down the hall. I nearly fainted when I saw a light shining in Chuck's bedroom. I knew I hadn't turned it on, and it surely hadn't come on by itself!

It was then that my curiosity got the better of me, and I took a step into the corridor. One step led to two, two to three, and pretty soon I found myself creeping stealthily along toward Chuck's open bedroom door. In my palms I clutched the poker. I held it upraised in readiness over my shoulder. If other noises had rippled from the room ahead, I hadn't heard them over the pulse beat thudding through my temples.

As I drew even with my buddy's doorway, a shadow shot across my path. With a horrific scream, I lunged forward and swung the poker with all my might. Somehow, I drew it back just before it stuck home in the middle of *Chuck's* face. At the same instant, *his* fist froze mid-flight six inches from my head. Tightly gripped in that fist were the deadly, long-bladed scissors from Mrs. Wilson's sewing basket.

I looked at Chuck. Chuck looked at me. The same murderous gleam reflected from our eyes. Finally, my friend's face softened into a smile, and he flung the scissors onto the bed. "If it isn't the late Mr. Wilson," he mumbled.

The next instant we were hugging each other and laughing hysterically. When I finally managed to control myself, I said, "What in God's name are you doing here? I thought you flew the coop with the rest of the chickens."

"I did," croaked Chuck sheepishly. "But I was in such a panic to get out of here that I didn't take the right books with me. With finals coming up, I thought I'd better come back for them. Why did you sneak up on me like that, anyway?"

"Why didn't you yell when you came in?"

"Gee, Bill, I'd didn't want to scare you."

Again, we broke into hysterics while my friend rushed over to his desk and snatched up his chemistry text and a psych book.

"And where do you think you're going with those?" I asked.

"Home, of course."

"And leave me here alone? Oh, no, you don't. I'm going with you."

"What about your research?"

"Believe me. It can wait!"

I ran to my room and tossed a couple of Henry James novels and some clothes in a gym bag. It wasn't until Chuck and I were safely in his car that I realized I still had the poker clutched in my hand. My pal must have noticed it about the same time, for he said, "I hate to disappoint you, Bill, but we don't have any ghosts at my house. Why don't you return that thing to Mrs. Wilson's living room before you hurt somebody with it?"

"If you go back inside with me and turn on the lights. . ."

Chuck smiled weakly before shifting into reverse. "On second thought," he muttered, "let's get the hell outta here!"

WHEN THE HUNTER
BECOMES THE HUNTED

The ridge grew appreciably steeper. Frank took two more weary steps and then plopped exhausted onto a fallen log. Despite his fatigue, there was a determined glimmer in his eyes, and his right hand never strayed far from the high-powered rifle cradled in the crook of his arm. Even clad in bulky hunting garb, the gaunt man looked like a stick figure against the background of snow.

The hunter glanced at his feet and contemplated his heavy, insulated boots. *No wonder I'm beat,* he thought. *I must be wearing at least twenty pounds of clothing. God, how does Boss keep up such a pace? Who does he think he is, anyway? Daniel freaking Boone?*

The man he had been tracking through the snow was chief architect at Wright's Construction Company and Frank's hated superior. His real name was Dwight M. Stone III, but everyone, including the owner of the company, called him "Boss." He had earned his nickname mainly through his gruff manner and the dread he instilled in his crew with his cold, amber eyes. Jimmy, the office clerk, best characterized their effect when he exclaimed after a nasty reprimand, "Sometimes Boss makes me feel like a roast cooking on a spit!"

What made Boss' hold over others complete was a powerful build that dwarfed that of even the most muscle-bound bricklayer on the payroll. Yet, the puzzling part was how he kept in such good condition. He didn't swim. He didn't pump iron at the Y. He didn't even play on the company's flag football team. And for someone who had no time for jogging, it was amazing how he had been able to stride up over this hogback without pausing once for a breather.

As Frank contemplated these mysteries, he glanced down the gully he had just scaled at the tangle of moss covered rocks and fallen logs that had sent him sprawling numerous times during his ascent. Unfortunately, the terrain ahead looked even more broken. The thickly wooded ridge rose steadily before leveling off into a laurel-choked hilltop. Stumbling to his feet, the hunter soon discovered that Boss' track, like those of some pursued beast, led off into the densest part of this thicket.

Frank lowered his head and bulled along thinking how foolish he had been to follow Boss. Jealousy, that's all it was! Jealousy and a desire to know what made him the most successful hunter at camp every year. So what if the SOB did choose to hunt alone? Was it a crime that he refused to take part in their drives or to even stand on point while deer where driven by him?

Yet, how nervous Boss always got the night before the hunt. The way he prowled about the camp keeping everyone awake, one would have thought he was the quarry. And that beard-growing ritual of his was equally ridiculous. While most guys didn't shave the weekend before buck season, Boss started his growth a whole month ahead of everyone else, saying it brought him luck. By the time the first day rolled around, his face was a mass of matted fur that concealed every feature but those damned amber eyes. If anything, they grew even more piercing as the day of the hunt drew nearer.

Frank paused to examine Boss' dim boot tracks. In the heart of the thicket, they had become increasingly difficult to follow. Besides the sheer density of the laurel, matters were complicated by the patches of bare granite protruding from the snow. In places Boss was able to go over fifty yards at a time without leaving a single track. When that happened, Frank was forced to circle until he again picked up the trail. Two-thirds the way through the tangle of brush, Frank lost it altogether. It was here that he found Boss' cap, coat, and rifle cached beneath a fallen hemlock.

"Damn!" muttered Frank as he examined the other hunter's gear. "What does Boss do, run down a buck and stab it to death with his knife?"

With his head bobbing like an agitated turkey, Frank glanced nervously into the thicket before chuckling grimly to himself. "Why, he can't do that! That's illegal! Maybe once I'm clear of this puckerbrush, I'll catch the stinking outlaw and turn him in. What will old man Wright think of his precious Boss then?"

Frank bolted through the remaining tangle of laurel, emerging totally spent. Toppling forward into the snow, he didn't even try to protect his rifle. When his dizziness passed, he opened his eyes and unsuccessfully scrutinized the ridge below him for Boss. It wasn't for several minutes that he noticed the huge set of canine tracks into which he had collapsed.

Frank scrambled to his haunches and examined the prints more closely. "What the hell?" he wondered aloud. "These are either the biggest dog tracks I've ever seen, or a wolf's! But there haven't been any wolves around here in over a hundred years. And those were Lobos, not the big timber variety. Man, these prints look like the ones I saw outside my sanitarium window."

As Frank rose to poke the snow from his rifle barrel, he felt very cold despite his recent exertion. Picking up the canine's fresh trail, he slunk along, eyes aglitter, scanning every patch of brush capable of hiding a red squirrel. Each time he paused to catch his breath, he kept his back against a tree and his gun ready to fire. *I'll bet this is exactly how Boss would proceed*, he thought.

The beast made no attempt to hide its track. Frank followed it with ease over the ridge and into a little hollow that was usually teeming with deer. Proof of that he found in the form of a badly mauled doe lying dead across the trail. Its throat was severed and sash marks bloodied its flank. Half-eaten entrails hung from a hole gnawed in its side. By the small amount of deer hair scattered about, Frank knew it couldn't have put up much of a struggle. Whatever had killed it, be it dog or wolf, had overpowered the poor doe with a strength Frank cared not to witness firsthand.

With a shiver, the hunter slipped his rifle off safe and backtracked until he had located the point of ambush. Frank soon discovered the imprint of the canine's body where it had lain upwind and above the well-traveled deer trail. He even saw where it had propelled itself onto the back of its prey. The funny part was, that's where its trail ended! There were plenty of hoof marks left by the staggering doe, but the big dog prints had absolutely vanished.

Frank fearfully inspected the hemlock branches around him and then backed slowly out of the hollow, his knuckles white on his gunstock. As he retreated up the ridge, his thoughts suddenly returned to Boss. *What if **he** should encounter this beast?* Frank gloated. *What chance would even Boss have? That'd fix the SOB for recommending me for psychological testing. I'd welcome the sight of him mutilated along the trail!*

Cackling to himself, Frank strode toward the thicket where several hours ago he had lost Boss' track. Although this route was tougher going, it would shorten his journey back to camp by at least an hour. With any luck, he might even get out of the woods before twilight faded from the gloomy December sky.

The hunter plunged frantically through the undergrowth, dogged by the lengthening shadows. The faster he hurried, the more he tripped over gnarled roots and slipped on broken granite. Soon, he was limping and drenched with sweat. When he had about reached the limit of his endurance, his senses were jarred by a series of hoarse grunts echoing from the laurel ahead.

Frank slid into the kneeling position and wrapped his sling around his left arm. Even that didn't steady his rifle as he sighted down the barrel in anticipation of the mad, snarling rush of the cur that now stalked *him*. He planned to fire at the last possible instant to insure the bullet's optimum shocking power. He dare not miss. In these close quarters, he may only hold together, long enough for one shot.

The brush rattled, and the hunter's finger tightened on the trigger. Just one more step. One more. . .

There was a grunt. The brush parted, and Frank's finger froze in mid-squeeze. Instead of a blood-crazed beast, out stepped Boss hauling behind him his latest trophy buck. Fixing the other man with his cold, amber eyes, he said, "Getting a little jumpy, aren't you, Frank? I didn't think they let you carry a gun anymore."

Flushing, the hunter lowered his rifle and got stiffly to his feet. He always felt five-years-old whenever Boss chided him. That was what made working for him such a strain. Especially annoying to Frank was Boss' habit of hovering over his drawing board whenever he worked with ink. How was anyone supposed to produce his best work with old Vulture Eyes leering at him?

"Nice b-b-buck," Frank finally stammered. "Where did you g-g-get him?"

"Over there," snapped Boss, jerking a thumb behind him. He was now fully clothed and had his own weapon slung over his shoulder.

"In the middle of all that laurel? Say. . .was that your stuff I found cached back there?"

"Yep, I found a cave I wanted to explore. The only way I could squeeze inside was to leave behind my coat and gun."

"What time did you s-s-shoot your buck?"

"Oh, I got him about a half hour ago."

"Funny. I didn't hear you f-f-fire."

"The wind must have been blowing in the wrong direction."

"M-m-maybe you're right. Let me get a closer look at those horns."

As Frank lurched forward, Boss stepped squarely in his path. "Oh, no," he growled. "You're not walking behind me with a loaded rifle. You'll have plenty of time to admire the buck's head when I get it mounted. It'll be hanging in the office soon enough with all the others. I'm surprised they let you come back to work after you pinned my hand to your drawing board with that damn compass. I wouldn't have sent you to Canada for a little *vacation*. I'd have put you away for good!"

"H-h-how do you know where the company s-s-sent me?" asked Frank, remembering those huge canine tracks outside the sanitarium.

"I have my ways. Now, back off!"

With a whimper, Frank withdrew after catching a glimpse of the dead deer. It had the same gnawed throat as the doe he had found down the trail.

"Boss, this may sound crazy, b-b-but did you see a. . .wolf. . .out here today?"

A smile spread over Boss' lupine face, and a flash of white teeth showed in his beard. "I think you should head back to camp now," he said in a condescending whisper. "I don't need any help dragging out my kill, and it will be dark soon. Yes. Very, very soon. . ."

THE GREAT STAG

The lone hunter slid noiselessly from a thicket of scrub beech and entered a path that wound up a steep mountain choked with brush and trees. The man was clad in a raveled blanket coat and a pair of stained wool pants. A knit cap was crammed over an unruly mop of bootblack hair. A smile played across his weather-cracked lips as he admired the fresh snowfall that made the day perfect for tracking and hunting. After adjusting the scoped rifle cradled in his left arm, he again set his gum boots in motion.

The half-breed worked methodically up the mountain. Often, he stopped to scan the woods around him for the elusive deer he stalked. Each time he paused, he put his back against a trailside tree to conceal his outline. Soon, he began to encounter fresh hoof prints that spilled from the mountainside across his path. That made him even more alert and slowed his pace to a veritable crawl.

The hunter inched his way along until spotting a distinctive, wide set of boot prints that entered the trail from a bisecting road. Glancing warily from left to right, he felt a sudden sweat pop out on his forehead. Before he could bolt for the nearest brush, a warden clad in dark green camo stepped out from behind a broad oak to block his escape.

"Where ya goin', Blackie Grimes?" demanded the officer, his hand straying toward the pistol housed on his hip.

"Uh. . .Feeggered I'd follow theze deer, Luke," muttered the half-breed, pointing toward a set of pronounced tracks veering up the slope.

"Yeah, right! Where's yer orange clothin'? After I give ya a warnin' an' a fine, ya know durn well that it's illegal to hunt without it."

"Right here, meester," grunted Grimes, turning to reveal a patch of faded blaze cloth stitched crudely to the back of his coat. "I'm wearin' two hundred feefty square eenches of orange. . .like the rule book says. You can measure eff you want."

"That don't cut it! You know as well as me that the orange must be visible from all directions. Looks like I get ta run ya in."

"But I's way legal," protested Blackie. "Lookee here."

The half-breed bowed toward Warden Luke. Atop his knit cap was pinned a scrap of reddish yellow yarn that technically fulfilled the limits of the law.

Grumbling to himself, the officer said, "The only difference 'tween you an' a coyote is that you smell worse. But you'll screw up. An' I know ya already done potted two deer."

"Even coyotes must eat!" snapped Blackie, forgetting the *five* bucks he had already shot. Fire blazed in his sullen eyes at the insult. He glared at the tall warden and tightened his grip on his gunstock.

"Yeah, but at least them predators know who's the big dog," growled the lawman, drawing himself up to his full height. "What are ya doin' in the woods anyhow if'n ya already killed two deer?"

"I has ze bonus tag," replied the half-breed, again turning to show Luke the extra license holder pinned on his back.

"Which en-titles ya ta one more doe. I'll be watchin' ya, Grimes. You best believe it!"

"Then, you best be able to drive ze truck to the top of that mountain," chuckled Blackie, motioning toward Luke's pickup that was half concealed by a patch of beech farther down the road. "That's whcrc I do ze good hunting."

"Ya don't think I can hike up there?" snarled the lanky officer. "Why, I can still walk the legs off a little runt like you any day o' the week, includin' Sunday. See ya at the the top. You bet!"

"See you in ze fires of hell!" yipped Blackie, giving the warden a mock salute and a thumb to the nose.

Before the lawman could bark back, Grimes leaped into the nearest thicket and bolted straight up a severe incline that most bears couldn't have climbed. Using saplings and branches for handholds, he struggled upward until he reached the next bench. There, he collapsed in the snow, listening to Luke's faint, windblown curses below.

When the half-breed's breathing returned to normal, he staggered to his feet and found another faint trail that wound around the mountain. Again, he assumed a hunter's stealth and crept along searching the woods with his piercing, pitch-colored eyes. He continued on until he reached the next trail that led steeply upward to the summit. There were deer tracks everywhere, and he licked his cracked lips knowing that he'd soon be among the fat doe that swarmed on the ridgetop.

Blackie's heart thudded with excitement when he spied a rusted oil tank capsized in the snow ahead. Just behind the overturned tank sat an abandoned powerhouse that marked the beginning of the best hunting territory. The building was made of tin, and its door yawned open to reveal a long-silent engine that once operated ten creaking rod lines and oil jacks. Now, the powerhouse provided winter refuge for skunks and other small critters. The half-breed grinned as he watched a startled squirrel dart inside. Then, he stomped toward the beech thicket that crowned the peak beyond.

Keeping to the trail, Grimes slunk through a sea of rattling, orange leaves. He moved a step at a time, keeping his eyes trained on the path ahead. He hadn't gone more than a quarter mile when he saw a doe's nose poke from the brush only fifty yards distant. To avoid detection, the hunter slipped into a prone position. He stared through his scope and snicked his rifle off safe.

The lead doe crept stiffly from the beech, sniffing the air for enemies. Cautiously, she peered in all directions before moving to the middle of the trail. Behind her were two yearlings that followed in trusting obedience. The herd had barely stepped into the open when the roar of Blackie's .30-40 Krag rent the silence with deadly thunder.

The doe's head exploded in a cloud of hair and gore, and she crashed unmoving to the ground. With stunned bleats, her young ones milled about, staring stupidly into the brush ahead with wild, panicky eyes. As they sidled side-by-side toward their downed mother, a second shot rang out. It was the last sound either of them was to hear. The bullet tore through the neck of the first yearling and then entered the second just above the front shoulder. Both small doe collapsed in a spray of blood to kick weakly and gurgle one last astonished cry.

Blackie was up and racing toward the deer the instant they fell from the crosshairs of his scope. "Show me a coyote that could do that," cackled the half-breed, still fuming over the warden's insult. "I kill with ze efficiency no beast can match!"

Grimes whipped out a wicked-looking skinning knife. He slit each deer's throat in turn to make sure they were good and dead. "Now, I got meat—'til strawberries make ze venison sweet again," he whispered, glancing warily down the trail toward the powerhouse. "Must hide theze. Queek! Luke must not see."

The half-breed dragged the mother doe over to a great gray beech blown down by a recent squall. He dug furiously in the snow beneath the trunk and then crammed the deer's carcass in the space he had created. Similarly, he concealed the body of one of the yearlings beneath a neighboring windfall. When he returned to the

93

road to fetch the second small doe, a flight of chickadees sailed from the brush and began circling Blackie's head. The birds beat their wings furiously, calling with angry "deedeedees." They closed within inches of the man's face, slapping at him with their feathers. Their attack was so fierce and persistent that Grimes was forced to drop his gun in the snow to cover his head with both arms. Again and again, the chickadees dove at him until finally he lashed out with a big mittened paw and knocked one of his antagonists from mid-flight.

"What ze hell is wrong with you?" howled the half-breed, stomping the chickadee beneath his gum boots. "Since when such happy birds go loco?"

The other birds continued to dive at Grimes, who danced and slapped like a honey bear beset by bees. They did not stop until one-by-one they were batted from the sky and trampled into bloody pulps.

Fuming and covered with sweat, Blackie hid the second yearling with her sister. Still distracted, he broke off a branch and brushed away his tracks that led to his deer caches. After wiping out signs of the does' demise from the snowy road, he stooped to pick up his rifle. Cursing in both English and Iroquois, he knocked the snow from the barrel. Next, he cleaned the lens of his scope with a soiled, blue handkerchief that he yanked roughly from his pants pocket. When the .30-40 Krag was safe to fire again, he grunted, "Too early to quit ze hunt. Still have bonus tag. Ha! Ha!"

Blackie cast several furtive glances down the trail behind him. Afterward, he prowled along the ridge looking for more venison on the hoof. His eyes had a murderous cast as he slipped noiselessly through the powdery snow. He skulked along, stopping often to survey the still winter woods. Finally, he paused by a patch of bloodred brambles to blow his nose. As he fished for the oft-used handkerchief, a scolding grouse erupted from the thicket inches from where Grimes stood. With a surprised gasp, the half-breed leaped back, lost his footing, and toppled to the ground. In the process, he cracked his skull on a rock. Then, a darkness descended as the rush of wings dissipated down a black slope.

After many minutes, Grimes' eyes fluttered open. His vision blurred when he attempted to raise his head, and he sank groaning back into the snow. It took him six tries before he could sit up. He finally fought to his feet and shook his fist in the direction the grouse had flown. "Doddamn you!" he growled. "I come back. With my shotgun I git you. Warden not always on patrol."

Grimes knocked the snow from his rifle a second time and lurched woozily forward. He hadn't taken more than a step or two when a pileated woodpecker gave a loud, warning cry. The alarm was immediately taken up by a red squirrel and then by blue jays as the half-breed slogged up the ridge. With so many creatures announcing his presence, Grimes stomped angrily through the snow. Finally, he broke into a wolf's lope to lose the pesky sentinels. He trotted and then sprinted with the sharp, reproving voices dogging him. On and on he raced, losing track of time and consciousness. The cries seemed to grow louder, the faster he ran.

Grimes continued up the trail until blackness crowded his vision. With a spent grunt, he fell on his face and lay motionless until a swirling wind revived him. When he crawled groggily to all fours, he found himself in a part of the forest he had never hunted. Here, the deadfalls lay buried beneath caskets of snow. Rotted beeches leered at him with knothole faces, and grave groves of hemlocks creaked in the breeze. A bad headache magnified this creaking until Blackie clamped his hands over his ears.

A stiff wind probed Grime's coat like icy corpse fingers. To escape its chill, he staggered to his feet and followed an oft-used deer trail into a wooded hollow below the ridgetop. There, he discovered fresh deer sign everywhere. Tracks crisscrossed the forest floor and led to widespread diggings made by hungry bucks and does. With acorns as thick as marbles beneath the disturbed snow, it was no secret to Blackie why so many deer congregated in this yard. He took a second to examine the lofty oaks that towered over him and then returned to his cruel business. Ignoring the pounding in his temples, he looked for a good point of ambush on a prominent crossing.

The half-breed had barely concealed himself behind a hemlock when a faint wailing reached his ears. He strained to listen until the cries of "Help! Help!" echoed from the ridge behind him. As the voices drew nearer, they assumed the high-pitched key of lost children. Finally, the carousel of haunted wails swirled directly overhead. With the sky alive with anguish, Blackie felt the gooseflesh rise on his extremities, and he hunkered closer to the trunk that sheltered him.

Doubting his own sanity, Grimes glanced upward and saw the boiling clouds part to reveal a broken flight of geese flailing the dark sky with their wings. Grinning uneasily, he snapped his rifle off safe and muttered, "So it's you who cause ze racket. Must be echo of hollow that makes you sound like leetle kids. I should shoot you down for scaring Blackie so!"

Still spooked, Grimes shifted his scrutiny to the deer crossing he hoped would bring him a huge buck. He had seen fresh scraping on every sapling he had passed since entering this mountain sag. By the length and breadth of these buck rubs, he knew they had been made by more than a spike or four point polishing its antlers. He licked his lips greedily at the thought of such a buck and tried to control the shaking that still made aiming his rifle a chore.

Grimes raised his .30-40 Krag and peered through the scope. Carefully, he looked down the trail to make sure he had a clear shooting lane. No sentinel birds gave him away this time as a foreboding silence gripped the entire wood. It wasn't long before he discerned the faint crunching of snow just below him to his left. With his pulse pounding in his ears, he raised his rifle again only to find the scope completely fogged. As he dug frantically for his handkerchief, the heavy footsteps of the approaching beast grew louder and louder and LOUDER.

Just as the head of a Great Stag popped over the rise, Blackie yanked his handkerchief free and began swabbing madly at his obscured lens. Not that he needed any magnification to see the massive rack bobbing toward him atop the hugest deer he had encountered in twenty years of hunting. The buck's back was a good five feet high, and his legs were big around as a draft horse's. Enraged grunts poured from the beast's brawny, white throat. Steam poured from its flared nostrils. Its eyes had a mad cast to them. The antlers appeared even more impressive with each powerful step the buck took. Blackie's mouth flew open in amazement when he counted twenty-five points on the sharp horns.

No matter how hard the half-breed rubbed his scope lens, he could not defog it. The stag now closed within fifty feet and dropped its head to charge the quivering hunter. With the pounding of hooves throbbing in his skull, Blackie whipped up his rifle and blindly yanked the trigger. Instead of the roar he expected, there was the sick thud of a firing pin striking a dud cartridge.

Before Grimes could chamber another round, the huge buck rose on its hind legs and lashed out with its left, front hoof. The blow smashed Blackie's nose to jam and shook the rifle from his quivering hands. As the hunter tottered, spewing blood, a swirling wind filled the hollow with a strange, priest-like chant. "I am Divine," it hummed. "I am Divine."

The buck punched with its other front hoof, knocking out Grime's teeth. As more gore squirted from his pulverized face, the half-breed suddenly remembered the three does he had slaughtered on the ridge. With a whimper, he dropped to his knees and raised his hands in a prayerful, pleading pose.

The Great Stag bent down and thrust its saber-like antlers through Blackie's chest. The next instant, Grimes was lifted flailing into the air. He gurgled as blood filled his lungs. Flung skyward like a broken scarecrow, he emitted a hollow, helpless shriek. He hit the ground heavily, staring wide-eyed at the snorting, outraged beast towering above him. Then, there was nothing but blackness as a flurry of hooves hammered him into the gory snow.

An hour later, a warden dressed in green camouflage slipped to the lip of the hollow. Luke had been following Blackie's footprints for miles, and he paused to catch his breath and listen to the creaking of the frozen trees.

"Ain't never knowed an Indian ta hunt a place like this," whispered the warden, noting the knothole faces glowering from a stand of rotted beech. "Grimes must be addled by the fall he took back yonder. . .or outta his stinkin' mind!"

To calm himself, the lanky warden concentrated on following the half-breed's boot tracks. They led him down a well-pronounced deer trail into the bowels of a dank oak grove interspersed with witch-haired hemlocks. There, the footprints were more difficult to follow, often disappearing among fresh deer diggings.

As Luke glanced about the spooky glen, a grim smile flickered on his face. He grinned again when he remembered the strange way he had found the does cached just beyond the powerhouse. He still could not believe, that in the middle of the day, a nocturnal owl had swooped and knocked off his hat. That forced him to stop where a faint spray of deer blood stained the trail. Then, some nuthatches squawked and carried on so in the underbrush that the officer went there to investigate. Just a single drop of gore near a half-swept boot print led to his discovery of the two yearlings. With that, the warden had enough evidence to lift Blackie's hunting license and keep him out of the woods for a very long time.

"Serves the bugger right!" muttered Luke with renewed enthusiasm. "Gonna love bustin' Grimes' be-hind once I catches up with 'im."

The lawman sneaked a little faster, taking long, silent strides through the snow. It had become eerily quiet, and he swore he heard the excited "deedeedees" of a ghostly flock of chickadees as he slipped along. Although he peered intently into the oak branches above him, he caught no glimpse of the black-capped birds.

Finally, the warden rounded a bend and found where Grimes' tracks came to an abrupt halt. At the exact moment he spotted a horribly mauled body, a blast of icy wind stabbed through his coat.

With chattering teeth, Luke bent to examine what was left of the poacher he had hunted for so long. Blackie's entire face was bashed in. His front teeth were missing. His nose was mashed gristle. One eye socket was vacant. The other housed an inky pupil bulged in unspeakable agony.

Luke turned and vomited into the snow. Wiping his mouth on his mitten, he continued his examination. It was then that he saw the jagged wound ripped by huge antlers the length of Blackie's chest.

"So a buck got 'im, eh?" grunted Luke. "An' here I figgered some ticked off landowner beat him to a pulp. The little bugger musta poured a whole bottle of doe scent on himself to get a buck so riled. Yet, I don't smell nothin'. . ."

The officer ran his hands over Grimes' rent ribs and on down his legs. Every major bone in his body had been shattered by what Luke concluded were wicked hoof blows. When the grunts of a buck resounded up the gully below him, he snatched a stout rope from his jacket pocket and tied a loop in one end. Feverishly, he worked the loop over the corpse's head, around his shoulders, and up under his armpits. Pulling the slipknot tight, he began dragging what was left of Blackie Grimes from the haunted hollow.

"No need ta get guys with a stretcher," muttered Luke, glancing nervously about. "Ain't e-nough left of Grimes fer that. Couldn't git no durned volunteers to come *here*, anyhow. . ."

Luke pulled for all he was worth as the wind kicked up to wash away his last words. Its swirling intensified until it assumed the howling pitch of a living thing. "I am Divine," the wind shrieked just as Luke saw a Great Stag step from behind a hundred-year-old oak to shake a huge set of horns stained with bright gore.

The warden didn't remember much after that. He lowered his head and charged uphill, his legs pumping like pistons. The exact moment the rope broke, he didn't know. Nor did he care what became of the corpse of Blackie Grimes. He had felt the breath of that Stag on the back of his neck and the breeze from those slashing antlers. All he knew is that he made it to the ridgetop. Yes, and now Luke could just see the old powerhouse ahead through a rattling screen of orange beech. He still didn't dare turn around. All he could do was run. Run for the road at the foot of this very scary mountain. The mountain that killed those who violated its laws and creatures.

THE HINSDALE HORROR

As Robert Dark Owl drove up the winding mountain road, he thought back to his visit with the shaman in Hinsdale. He had come to research his ancestry and learn why a whole village of Senecas—men, women, and children—had been murdered by others of their tribe. He had read often about the slaughter of the Iroquois by General John Sullivan in 1779 during the American Revolution, but why would his own people kill one another?

According to the shaman, the Senecas at Hinsdale had become very prosperous through trading with the Europeans and because of some extraordinary luck. It seems that they caught more fish, shot more game, and grew better crops than other Iroquois in the region. They also committed an unnamed "transgression" that led to their extermination.

Robert fidgeted in the driver's seat of his battered Ford pickup. He was a barrel-chested

Indian with sad, dark eyes and long, black hair worn in the style of his people. After stretching his tense muscles, he gripped the steering wheel with new resolve and turned onto a dirt road to the right.

The road dipped sharply before rising toward a wooded hilltop. Robert shifted gears and turned left onto a driveway that wound around the base of the hill. He drove through an overgrown field toward a tall pine a hundred yards distant. Just as he reached the wind-tossed tree, the driveway curved toward a white house that sat isolated and drear. In bad need of a paint job, the dwelling had a poorly patched roof and a busted upstairs window. Robert felt a chill pass through him when the curtains inside the broken window parted and then fell back together.

The couple who owned the house said they were harassed by animal apparitions and lamps that attacked them. When their children woke up covered with burn marks the day before, they had fled back to town to stay with relatives. They were more than happy to rent the place to Robert for the month of June. Their ashen faces and involuntary twitching testified to the fright they had experienced.

Exhausted from his long trip from Central Pennsylvania, Robert parked beside the low end of the house. Grabbing his duffel bag from the bed of his truck, he stomped onto a rickety porch and unlocked the front door.

Inside, he found an old-fashioned kitchen that spoke of a hasty retreat by the prior residents. A half-eaten breakfast still sat on the table, and chairs were thrown back in chaotic fashion. The refrigerator door was flung wide open, and its contents gleamed inside. There was a carton of eggs, two gallons of milk, and assorted pickle, relish, and mustard jars. Robert added some food of his own before shutting the door tight.

The big Indian then trudged into the first floor bedroom that was a picture of disarray. He placed his belongings in a ransacked dresser as he stared at clothes, games, and magazines strewn about the floor. There was also a Black Sabbath record sleeve tossed on the pile. The cover featured a green skinned witch who stood in front of a stone manor. Sunset glinted from fall foliage and an eerie black tarn. Robert had heard the album long ago and was spooked by the memory of its doom-laden, heavy chords and wailed lyrics.

With sleep crowding his eyes, Robert collapsed into an unmade bed. Not bothering to take off his clothes, he stretched out on the mattress, boots and all, and was snoring moments later. He dozed fitfully for an hour before waking in a sweat. The temperature in the house had become stifling, and the Indian caught a whiff of smoke. When he saw it billowing from the kitchen, he bolted through the doorway just in time to watch the sooty air transform into a huge gray wolf. The wolf fixed Robert with its yellow eyes and then leaped through the solid oak door.

Unnerved by the encounter, Dark Owl put a pot of coffee on to boil. There would be no sleep that night, so he sat at the kitchen table to pray to the Great Spirit for protection. He took a beaded medicine bag and a crucifix from his pocket and placed them in front of him as he entreated. His prayers continued until the first rays of daylight gleamed in the window and his last sip of coffee was gone.

Rising to his feet, Robert walked outside and took a deep breath of cool air. "According to the shaman, my answer lies within 250 feet of this house," he muttered. "That's where my ancestors are buried and the reason for my trip. Let it be an inner journey, as well."

Robert took 250 paces from the front porch into the dewy field ahead. His pant legs were soaked before he accomplished the task, but he paid his wetness no mind. With intense concentration, he began circling the house. He knew the Iroquois buried their dead in an upright position, so he scanned the ground for telltale mounds of earth. When he found no trace of a cemetery in the field, he entered the woods at the base of a steep hill.

Dark Owl had no sooner stepped into the shadowy tree line when he was beset by a swarm of gnats that blinded and befuddled him. Then, he heard a vague chanting echo from the hillside above. The monotone voices were somber and strange and repeated the same word again and again. The gnats' fierce buzz kept him from distinguishing what the choir sang.

The voices were hushed by the screech of a hawk, and the insects mutated into fog. Robert now found himself in a graveyard ringed by dark hemlocks. Instead of individual grave sites, he tottered on the brink of a mass burial pit sunk into the damp earth. Shards of pottery and clay pipes protruded from the soil along with bones and leering skulls.

While Robert surveyed the grim scene, blood bubbled suddenly from the ground. With a shriek he raced from the woods as branches raked his face and knocked him sideways. He trampled mayapples and bitter-smelling ferns in his mad scramble. Pursued by disembodied voices, he tore across the yard and on into the house.

Robert stood panting with his back to the door that he had somehow banged shut behind him. Immediately, the windows began opening and closing in the living room. He could hear them through the archway to his left. The slamming became more violent until the sound of shattered glass forced him to investigate. When he entered the room, the windows were still intact, but on the rug beneath them lay the ace of spades.

The hair elevated on Dark Owls' head as he cried out to the Great Spirit for deliverance. All grew silent with his prayer, and he began to pace and ponder. His pacing continued until mid-afternoon when weariness from his sleepless night overcame him. After one last look around, he fell on the couch and lapsed into a heavy slumber.

Robert woke with a splash of sunlight on his face. As he fought to escape the hot glare, he saw above him a flint-tipped arrow pointed at his throat. With a surprised yelp, he dove from the couch just as the arrow hissed through the air and buried itself where his neck had rested. Gibbering with fear, he scrambled to his knees only to find the arrow had vanished.

Dark Owl leaped up to flee the room when he heard a tapping on the window behind him.

Whipping around, he saw a collage of misty faces peering at him through the glass. Some were Indians. Others were tree bark creatures. All had hollow eyes, especially the children who stuck out their tongues to taunt him.

"Shadow People, be gone!" implored Robert. Instead, HE ran into the kitchen and ripped open the door.

As Robert dashed toward his truck, the haunted ones stared out every window at him. Their voices rose in a droning chant that was plain as a rumble of thunder. Over and over they roared, "Segoewa't'ha. Segoewa't'ha. Segoewa't'ha!"

"The devil!" shrieked Robert as he fumbled to unlock his truck. "My ancestors worshiped the DEVIL!"

Diving behind the steering wheel, Dark Owl turned the key and slammed the gas pedal to the floor. Instead of peeling backward from the driveway like he expected, the engine exploded in a fearful cloud of black smoke and flames. The blast blew open the hood, disabling his vehicle and jumbling his brain. Babbling nonsense, he watched the evil ones pour from the house. Then, the faces crowded around him, leering and sneering, until not one ray of sunlight entered the cab of his Ford.

THE PRICE OF A PINT

The hobo rubbed his arms and muttered incoherently as he glanced toward a trash bin overflowing with greasy newspapers and broken cardboard boxes. Even if he bedded down there again tonight, he'd probably freeze to death, for this was the coldest November ever. According to the flashing sign outside the Tenth Avenue Bank, it was already one degree below zero at six p.m. What he really needed was a little "antifreeze" to brace himself against the cold.

But how was he, Raymond Bartholomew, to afford such a luxury as the price of a pint? With heating bills on the rise, people just weren't as generous as they'd been last summer. Lately, a whole week's panhandling barely netted enough for an occasional cup of coffee. Even worse, business was so slow in most restaurants that they weren't hiring dishwashers. Without that money, he'd even lost his bed at the flophouse.

Raymond began to pace furiously back and forth across the alley he now called home. His face was a blur of tangled whiskers, and his hair protruded wildly from beneath a clownish bowler hat. His once fashionable suit was stained and tattered. With layers of grime caked on his skin, he looked vaguely Negroid lurking in the shadows.

There was always the possibly of a discrete mugging or two to keep a fellow going, but Raymond was much too squeamish for that. Besides, the only people weak enough for him to handle were either school children or senior citizens. Over the years he'd treated too many of those folks to find harming them palatable.

Raymond dug his freezing hands deep into his pockets and wandered onto Tenth Avenue. As he stumbled past a row of dark store fronts, he stared through their barred windows at the same warm overcoats and luxurious sweaters that had once hung in his own closet. Finally, he came to a halt in front of Falcon Brothers' Liquors. It was the only place on the block still open, and the warm lights glowed inside like an expensive whiskey at the bottom of a crystal tumbler.

The hobo opened the front door and slipped into the shop. Casually, he examined several shelves of gift liquors in colored bottles while casing the joint. The proprietor, a burly bare-armed man, had risen when he came in and was now studying him in the ceiling mirror just overhead.

Raymond sidled around a display of dinner wines and proceeded up the brandy aisle. Glancing into the mirror, he saw that his every movement was being logged by the big hulk behind the cash register. Oh well, if he couldn't swipe a pint, at least he was going to take his time and get warm.

Raymond spent a good ten minutes peering at the various brands and flavors of brandy—a liquor of which he had recently been a connoisseur. When his hands finally began to thaw, he reached out to "inspect" a preferred bottle more closely. His fingers had no sooner closed around it when a heavy paw thumped down on his shoulder.

"May I help you?" growled a voice close to his ear.

"Just looking," Raymond replied with a twitchy smile. "I see you have my favorite brandy in stock."

"Gee, am I ever relieved to hear that. Would you like to *buy* a bottle to take with you?"

"Uh. . .Yes, I would, but. . .unfortunately I forgot my wallet at home."

"Yeah, I know. And your broker's out of town, too."

Rough hands seized Raymond by the collar and the seat of his pants, and he was given the bum's rush out into the street. He skipped nimbly across the sidewalk until crashing headlong into a trash barrel set out along the curb. When he came to moments later, he found himself sprawled in the gutter covered with coffee grounds and rotted fruit.

Not bothering to brush himself off, Raymond wobbled to his feet and returned to the liquor store. Damn! His assailant hadn't even waited to see how much damage he had done. He was back behind the cash register ogling a girly magazine.

Raymond staggered away from the door and started down the block. His vision was blurry, and his lips felt swollen. What was he to do?

Wiping the corner of his mouth, he came away with his palm smeared with blood. "God, and all along I thought I was slobbering on myself again," he muttered. "What a waste of good blood. What a. . . Hey! That's it! That's it!"

Raymond quickened his pace as he entered a dingy neighborhood comprised mainly of tenement houses. This was the dark side of the city unlit by streetlights or the hope of salvation. Only the most desperate sort of white man dared venture here, and Bartholomew cringed as shadows flitted past him reeking of day-old whiskey and vomit cologne. Several times he heard shrieks emit from the bowels of an adjacent alley. Then, he understood why people turned their heads and walked away from daylight stabbings.

Three blocks into the darkness, the hobo came to a low, professional-looking building illuminated by a single bulb over the doorway. He pressed the buzzer, and a nurse appeared on the other side of a barred window. She stared cautiously past him into the street. Seeing he was alone, she opened the door latch electronically and motioned for him to enter.

Raymond found himself in the shadowy anteroom of Roma Corporation, one of a dozen metro companies that bought and sold blood. The need for such firms always existed in a city of two million people, for there were never enough donors to meet the needs of a diseased population prone to violent accident and heinous crime.

111

What is more, Roma and its counterparts weren't too particular about the type of scabrous lowlife from which they obtained their blood supply. Filling the quota was always the bottom line. If they had to set up headquarters in the middle of a ghetto, so be it.

The same nurse who had admitted Raymond to the premises emerged from behind a hospital screen and sat at a cluttered desk. Producing an official-looking form, she nodded toward a metal folding chair. Her movements were brisk, and her eyes were as sympathetic as flint. When Raymond was seated, she snapped, "Name?"

"Raymond Bartholomew."

"Address?"

"Uh. . .Tenth Avenue."

"Have you given blood in the past month?"

"No."

"Have you been out of the country recently?"

"No."

"Are you presently taking any medication?"

"No."

"Do you have hepatitis, syphilis, AIDS, or other communicable disease?"

"No."

"Have you drunk alcoholic beverages in the past week?"

"No."

"Okay, make your mark here and go down the hall to your right."

"Wait a minute," said Raymond coldly. "I'm very capable of *signing* my name."

"Then, *sign* here."

"Before I do, I'd like to know what this is for."

"It's a simple release," droned the nurse. "Will you hurry up? I haven't got all night!"

Bartholomew approached the desk, snatched up a pen, and scribbled his signature. During the entire interview, the nurse hadn't looked at him once.

"Before I go through with this, how much will I be paid?"

"Between thirty and forty dollars. It depends on your blood type. Will you make up your mind?"

Swallowing hard, Raymond nodded his assent and then passed along a darkened corridor and through a pair of swinging doors. He emerged into a large, well-lit room furnished with padded tables. Several of these were occupied by elderly residents of the ghetto.

Oh, well, thought Raymond as he glanced nervously about. *At least I'll get top dollar for my Type O blood.*

An ugly black nurse approached Raymond and led him to the nearest table. She instructed him to take off his coat, roll up his sleeve, and lie down. She scurried to a medicine cabinet, returning momentarily with a needle, a hose, a tourniquet, a plastic bottle, and a container of rubbing alcohol. She wrapped the tourniquet around Raymond's arm and gave it a couple of twists. Then, without warning, she sterilized a spot on his forearm and rammed the needle home. Before he could even yelp, she withdrew and reburied it a second time. She tried twice more to hit a vein before calling out in frustration to an elderly nurse. By that time, her patient had become strangely pale beneath the coats of grime on his face.

A testy white woman stormed over to Raymond's table and jerked the needle from the other nurse's hand. "Why can't they send me anyone but student nurses?" she raged as she successfully tapped a vein with one vicious poke of the needle. At that moment, Raymond must have lost consciousness, for later he couldn't remember watching them hook up the plastic sack into which his blood was dripping.

Bartholomew closed his eyes, but the nightmare didn't go away. No matter how many liquor bottles he conjured in his mind, he couldn't blot out the stale smell of urine wafting from the black fellow next to him.

God! Life is so unfair, reflected Raymond. *To look at me now, who'd believe that only last fall I examined patients on padded tables? Washing dishes isn't very satisfying after twelve years of college, medical school, and specialized training in pediatrics. Nor is being a social outcast for that matter. . .*

But how else was I to determine if the girl had VD? Of course, I should have never agreed to treat her without first notifying her parents. That was stupid! Yet, when you deliver a child into the world and see her through the measles, mumps, and chicken pox, you do feel responsibility toward her. I should have been less concerned about her embarrassment and more concerned for my own reputation.

Still, I can't believe she got sexual satisfaction from a simple medical exam, as she later claimed. A little rich girl might say anything, though, to keep from losing her allowance. Why should she care that I got expelled from the A.M.A for sexually deviant behavior with a minor and would never practice medicine again?

The other patient began to moan softly, and Raymond peeked in his direction. The old Negro was gripping his arm just above where the needle protruded from it. With sweat shimmering on his black skin, he reminded Raymond of a stereotypical slave from a second-rate Civil War movie. The only difference was that his master, the ghetto, hadn't needed whips and chains to inflict the required amount of suffering.

Raymond studied the needle sticking from his own arm. *I still must be in shock,* he reasoned. *Otherwise, wouldn't I feel pain? Just think how many blood samples I took without once considering how frightening it was for the patient. Oh well, at least tonight I'll return to the liquor store and buy **two** pints of brandy. Won't that clerk be surprised to see me again? Maybe the SOB will even apologize when I flash a little green. Then, I'll get a hotel room and sleep until noon under **real** sheets. And won't a nice hot bath feel good? And a shave? Why, I'll even get my suit cleaned and pressed. Then, I'll look like a proper—*

"Hey, mista! You! Hey!"

Raymond woke with a start and discovered his ugly black nurse hovering over him. She was tapping his shoulder impatiently while glancing at her watch.

"Yo time's up," she growled, "an' you won't git paid."

"Excuse me?"

"Look at yo sack, mista. You ain't but half filled it. Didn't they tell ya we only pays for a full unit?"

115

"You mean if I don't give a whole pint, I don't get any money?"

"That's right! Looks like we's just gonna have to pack it back in ya."

"Pack what back in me?"

"Yo blood. Now, you lay still. This is gonna hurt some."

The nurse raised the plastic sack even with her head, and the blood began flowing back down the long tube. The hobo winced and grabbed his arm. This time shock did little to dull the pain. When the sack was empty, the nurse yanked the needle free and slapped a band-aid over the still oozing hole. Pointing to the side exit, she said, "Okay, you can go."

"Go?"

"Are you deaf besides bein' a po bleeda? I said git outta here!"

Suddenly, Raymond felt very angry. He had gone through a lot for the price of a pint, and he wasn't going to be cheated. Brushing aside the nurse, he rushed over to a cart loaded with fresh blood. Before the staff could recover, he tore open a container and chugged it in one gulp.

By the time Raymond had finished his second bottle, the entire room was in an uproar. Nurses were screaming, buzzers were ringing, and patients were bellowing like bulls. Then, one old black man dove under a table, dislodging the needle from his arm. In seconds, the floor gushed with blood squirting from his plastic sack.

The head nurse rushed through the swinging doors in response to the alarm bell. Spotting Raymond, she wasted no time. With a grunt, she hurled herself at him, planting her fingernails in the middle of his back.

116

Bartholomew shrugged her off as if she were an opinion with which he disagreed. There was a strange gleam in his eye. His mouth was rimmed with crimson. In a single bound, he hurdled the table between him and the side exit. In another, he was out the door. Tenth Avenue was soon to become a very unsafe place for weak, warm-blooded beings.

FETTERS AND CHAINS

Jason came from a very unloving family. Although he was an only child, his parents were too busy despising each other to pay him much mind. His most vivid childhood memories were of sullen faces, threatening fists, and constant bickering. It is no wonder, then, that at a very early age, Jason decided marriage was a trap to be avoided at all costs.

In accordance with this resolution, Jason spent his early teenage years avoiding the opposite sex. Sure there were moments when a hint of perfume or the curve of girlish hips would arouse in him the vague animal lust peculiar to the pubescent male. But those lapses were always short-lived, for his built-in defense mechanism would conjure pinched images of his mother's owlish face so grotesque that he would turn away in disgust from the object of his longing.

Strangely enough, it was this very aloofness that made Jason most appealing to those he sought to evade. Also, by the time he was seventeen, he had become so darkly handsome, with his flashing black eyes and chiseled features, that every girl in his class longed to be the one to unlock the mysterious brooding that possessed him.

At first, Jason was puzzled by the alluring glances of the girls who sized him up as he took his seat in science or math class. When the awful truth finally dawned on him, he reacted like all true masters of any game—he used his knowledge to conquer and destroy his opponent. Naturally, being so young, Jason saw these objectives in purely sexual terms.

So began a long string of girlfriends whom he found, unwrapped, and unwound. If this sounds a bit formulaic, it was meant to be, for Jason developed a foolproof strategy of cold manipulation.

Invariably, each of Jason's encounters began when he permitted the female to make the first move. This gave his "prey" a false sense of security while, at the same time, making *him* appear vulnerable until he had gained the girl's complete trust. That usually didn't take long, considering his natural cunning and facility with the tender phrase. As one of the bereaved young ladies was to remark after his disappearance, "Jason could charm Cleopatra out of the arms of Anthony."

Another useful tactic Jason learned after two or three romances was to keep his woman off guard through a mixture of sweetness and cruelty. As a matter of fact, it seemed that she became hooked on him even sooner if he was lackadaisical about returning her phone calls or avoided her in the halls at school. It was also this same enigma that made it doubly hard for him to dispose of a babe once he had had his way with her. Each abuse he heaped upon his old lover made her want him twice as much. Little did she understand that his strained conversation and paleness were merely manifestations of the human animal balking from a trap.

Despite all the turmoil caused by his love life, Jason's senior year in high school went very well until a couple of weeks before the prom. At the time he was "between girls" and available. He had to decide which of the host of willing beauties should be given the privilege of taking him to the dance. He had narrowed it down to a pair of luscious juniors (who had been in hot pursuit for months) when the most peculiar thing occurred one morning before homeroom.

As was his custom, Jason was strolling down the hall "taking inventory." He was so intent upon rating each girl he passed—noting her figure, face, and future possibilities—that it took him awhile to realize he, too, was under scrutiny.

Fearing that a teacher had guessed his game, he wheeled stiffly around, half expecting to discover a ferret-faced adult behind him. Instead, he found himself examining the shapeliest chick he had ever seen. Such a judgment was easy to make, considering she stood framed in a sunlit doorway which revealed every shadowy curve of her body through her dress. Ironically, the same dazzling glare that highlighted her figure also masked her cocked face in a blinding aura of amber light.

As Jason noted every delicious inch of the girl's body, he became instantly aroused. He attempted to compliment her with his old line but found his throat so unnaturally constricted that he was unable to speak. Utterly disarmed by desire, he felt almost naked himself. In fact, he was so uncomfortable that he never questioned why such a dainty girl wore a spiked chain bracelet more befitting Hell's Angels than a high school coed.

At last, the girl shot Jason a dazzling smile. Numbly, he began babbling disjointed phrases that could have made no possible sense to anyone but her. When he walked away in a daze, even he could only recall that the chick's name was Hester and that *he* had asked *her* to the prom. Although he could not distinctly recall seeing her face, it's doubtful he could have resisted anyway.

On the night of the big dance, Jason was uncharacteristically apprehensive. He stayed locked in his bedroom all evening, adjusting his tux and fussing over his appearance. Finally, with the eighth chime of the hall clock ringing in his head, he stomped downstairs to hiss goodbye to his parents. He was especially uncivil to his mother when she dropped his date's corsage while fetching it from the refrigerator. His father's joke about him looking like a "stiff in a monkey suit" went over about as well. But who were they? Let them wallow in their ugly world.

Even behind the wheel of his old man's car, Jason couldn't relax. Nothing playing on the radio satisfied him, and he skipped from station to station. He wondered why he had not seen his date since that first morning. It seemed just plain unnatural that she hadn't phoned him or, at least, waited around for him after school. Was it possible that she actually planned to stand him up? How foolish he would look if he went to the biggest social event of the year with no lady hanging on his arm.

Only visions of Hester's sweet, shadowy figure kept Jason from totally panicking as he turned onto Denison Street and speeded toward the address the girl had given him during their only encounter. Could it be that she actually lived in such a ramshackle neighborhood? Had he not been so driven by lust, he certainly wouldn't have stayed to find out once he spied her soot-blackened apartment house dwarfed by the smokestacks of a nearby meat processing plant. As it was, he barely noticed the reek of old blood from the slaughterhouse next door when he boiled from his vehicle and charged up the front steps.

With his pulse thundering in his temples, Jason tapped lightly on the front door. Although it was a muggy May night, his teeth chattered and his eyes had a vague, glazed look about them. He was forced to rap more vigorously before he heard the clatter of high heels approaching from inside.

Finally, the door creaked open, and Jason was blinded by a flash of light. Only Hester's enticing voice told him he was indeed at the right address. He did not step inside until her hot fingers closed around his wrist like a set of manacles.

When the boy's eyes had adjusted to the glare, he found himself standing in a cavernous living room, the entire back wall of which was dominated by a blazing fireplace. A mantle lined with strange, ebony curios ran the full length of this wall. Before the fireplace was a circle of furniture made of polished black oak. The chairs and settees glistened with such brilliance they appeared to generate their own light.

Then, Jason's gaze lit upon Hester where she stood with firelight dancing on her face. Her own eyes were coyly downcast, and a smile played across her full, supple lips. She was attired in a black, sequined gown that sparkled seductively with her every move. Its plunging neckline attracted Jason like a thief is drawn to a strand of pearls.

Sensing her advantage, Hester ensnared Jason in her arms and led him in an enchanted waltz around the chamber as soft music began to play. Jason was so bewitched by the sensual nature of this melody that he lost track of the course their dance followed across the living room and down an adjacent hallway. Then, Hester released her embrace, retreated a step, and slipped her dress off her shoulders and onto the floor. All thoughts of the prom slipped from Jason's mind, as well.

Jason blinked in amazement as he drank in every slinky curve of the girl's naked form. At last, he realized they were in a dimly-lit bedroom, and that she was motioning for him to lie back on the waterbed behind him. When she saw he was too numb to respond, she took his hand and ran it across the satin coverlet over the bed. This simple act brought him unspeakable pleasure and promised even more.

With a recklessness only carnal lust can produce, Jason tumbled backward and reached out his hand for his lover. He hit the coverlet with a sploosh that made the gooseflesh thick on his buttocks. The next instant, he felt himself sinking in a benumbing tank of murky liquid. He was completely out of breath by the time he touched bottom, shoved off with one foot, and propelled himself to the surface. When he broke water, he was greeted by his first real glimpse of Hester's eyes.

A scream rattled from Jason's throat, and he sank a second time. With the freezing water deadening his limbs, it felt like an eternity before he again hit bottom. When his left foot finally did touch, a pair of jaws clamped shut around his ankle. Sharp teeth tore at his flesh, and a cloud of blood bubbled upward past his face. In an animal frenzy, he kicked and thrashed until a lack of oxygen choked the fight out of him. Only as Jason settled to the floor of the tank, did he see the bear trap that secured him.

Meanwhile, two crimson pupils peered expectantly downward into the dank pool. Just as the water quit bubbling, the faint buzz of a doorbell echoed from down the hall. Hester glanced once more into the water to note a second tap and then pulled the satin coverlet in place over the bedframe. As she left the room, her hellish eyes were cast coyly downward. Her formal gown glistened with each delicious movement of her hips.

THE ONE AND ONLY PRICE VINCENT

The guitarist bent scowling over his instrument. He had stayed up all night to compose a song, and it was easy to tell by the sullenness of his eyes that he was far from satisfied with the results. As he strummed the catchy chords over and over, his mind fumbled vaguely for some suitable lyrics.

Just as the guitarist was about to give up in frustration, the front door swung open and in strode a bearded young hipster with several sheets of typing paper clutched tightly in his hand. He brought with him from the street the echoes of a waking city.

"What's shakin', dude?" asked the visitor. "Hey, that sounds like a really happenin' tune you're workin' on."

"Yeah, Willard," grunted the guitarist with a thin smile. "It's gonna be a million-seller. I just know it."

125

"You've hit on a good riff, all right. Say, if ya haven't got any lyrics yet, why don't ya take a look at these, Price? I like wrote all five of 'em last night before I crashed. Talk about a creative burst!"

Willard perched on a stool next to Price Vincent and handed him the neatly typed lyric sheets he had gotten up early to prepare. With surprise, he noted the hard look that passed over the guitarist's face when he snatched them up.

"Hey, Price, from the part of your song I heard, I think the words to my 'Hannah' will fit it perfectly. Check it out, dude!"

Vincent leafed through the pages until he found the lyrics Willard was so enthused about. Halfheartedly, he skimmed through them before tossing aside his partner's work. As the lyric sheets rained to the floor, he sprang from his stool and slammed his instrument into its case. He was careful Willard did not see the jealous hatred burning in his eyes when he bolted for the control room.

After Price had stomped away, Willard snatched up one of the scattered sheets and followed after him. "Hey, you didn't tell me what you thought of 'Hannah,' " he blared, laying his lyric on the control board where the musician would be sure to see it. "If you don't like that one, I'll be glad to help you revise whatever you've started."

"Don't be so damn pushy!" snapped Vincent. "I'm nearly finished, and I don't need *your* help!"

"Hey, what's wrong with you lately, man? It seems like every time I make a suggestion, you snap my head off."

"Don't you think I'm capable of writing my own lyrics? Didn't I compose the band's first hit, 'Rivers of Blood?' "

Willard leaned against a filing cabinet and stared hard at his friend, who hovered over the control board with his back toward him. Price's shoulder-length hair concealed the sides of his face, shielding the dark thoughts that lurked there.

"Hey, why won't you work with me anymore?" squeaked the lyricist. "I wrote the words to over fifty songs in the past six months, and you've only used one of them."

To emphasize his point, Willard jerked open the bottom drawer of the filing cabinet and revealed a veritable treasure trove of his material. "Why do you think I've penned all of these? For the sake of mental exercise? Look at me, man!"

Price mumbled something under his breath but did not turn around.

"Man, you know I write topnotch stuff! After all, haven't I won prizes for my work in international competitions? Haven't I?"

The guitarist stiffened at his partner's bluster. Willard had been bragging about those prizes for months. In an effort to keep his cool, Vincent snatched up a screwdriver and began drumming it against the face of the control board. *If only Willard would shut up*, he thought. *I'm much too tired to deal with this hassle now. I need sleep, bad. I—*

"Price, I need to know now! When do you plan to start using my material again? Don't forget that I've been doing the grunt work for you and the Electrocutioners for like eight years. Yeah, from the beginning, I was your lyricist,

127

roadie, and publicity agent. Now, that we're on the verge of stardom, it seems like a poor time to cut me out. Sure your one song was our first hit single, but you don't have to be greedy. How do you expect me to benefit financially if you don't release any of my material? After all the hard work I put into this band, I deserve better!"

The guitarist still did not answer. Instead, he surveyed the outer studio through the Plexiglas window above the control board. As he noted the stack of amplifiers piled next to the front door in readiness for that night's gig, he thought about how much sweat and money he himself had funneled into the band. Had he not taken out personal loans for the equipment truck, PA system, and studio recording deck? Had he not—

"Hey, Price, hey! Answer me!" shouted Willard into his partner's ear. He was now so furious that his voice rose to a piercing, obnoxious pitch. There was also a nasty gleam in his eyes as he continued: "Price, if you're not reasonable about this, I'm left with no alternative. You know how the copyright forms include each author and his contribution? Well, if you remember, we weren't required to tell which individual songs were co-written and which were not. That means as far as the boys in Washington are concerned, I helped you with every single tune on our last copyright tape. Yeah, I'm gonna swear I'm the co-author even if you did write all but one song yourself. Dig?"

Price's eyes widened in acknowledgment. "Like hell!" he roared, turning to bury the screwdriver he'd been fingering into his partner's throat.

Surprise gurgled from Willard's crushed voice box. Then, he toppled backward, blood spurting from the hole in his larynx. With his last gasp of breath he watched horrified as Price grabbed "Hannah" from the control board and torched it with his lighter.

A vicious leer burned on Vincent's face while he watched the typed lyric sheet burn down to his fingertips. He dropped the charred embers to the floor and furiously stomped them out. Then, he glanced madly about the studio, chanting, "What to do with the body? The body. The body. What to do with the body? Now that I freed its dark soul! Why, that's it! The lyrics I searched for all night! Yeah, what can I do with you, Willard, now that I've released your soul?"

It was minutes before show time, and electricity surged through the air. While Price adjusted his guitar strap, he glanced across the darkened stage toward the shadowy figures of roadies who scurried back and forth moving monitors and setting up mic stands. Red amplifier eyes and lit cigarettes glowed in the murk. Although Price couldn't distinguish the drummer, he knew he was behind his kit by the tattoo of drum sticks rattling from snare to tom to cymbal and back again. As he listened to the primal beat, he quivered with the excitement felt by boxers before a championship bout. After all, wasn't performing life's ultimate high?

When two shadows glided toward their microphones to Price's right, he strode to his amplifier and plugged in his guitar. At that moment the audience flickered with the gleam of a thousand lighters held head-high by the impatient crowd. He was about to join his bassist center stage when the head roadie grabbed him by the arm and whispered, "Hey, Price, have you seen Willard? He's supposed to run the follow spot tonight."

"Yeah, he's around here somewhere, but I doubt he'll be much help."

"Why not?"

"He's been having some trouble with his throat."

"What does that have to do with him manning the follow spot?" grumbled the roadie.

"Hey, that's not my problem! Do the best you can!" snarled Vincent as he shook himself free from the other's grasp. "Willard may show up later, but I doubt it."

Before the roadie could protest further, there was a blinding burst of light. Flash pots exploding near the front of the stage bathed the band in eerie crimson. The audience squealed with unbridled delight when the M.C. shouted above the din, "Ladies and gentlemen, it is with great pleasure that on behalf of the Fairfield College student government, I present the one and only Price Vincent and the Electrocutioners!"

Right on cue, Price leaped into the spotlight that appeared center stage. Cranking his guitar to five, he laid down some nasty licks. With the rest of the band blasting away behind him, he danced and gyrated like a madman undergoing electroshock therapy. He did a split at the exact moment the stage again erupted with flash pot fire.

The louder the audience howled its approval, the louder Vincent cranked up his guitar. By midway through the set, he had the dial turned to eight as he boogied through the Rolling Stone oldie, "Satisfaction." He and his bassist bumped to the beat while pumping their instruments in a suggestive fashion. When the rhythm section settled into a pulsing groove, Price screamed into the microphone, "Have any of you people ever loved someone who wouldn't even fart in your face? Well, I have!"

"Me, too," chirped the bassist, "and it ain't no fun!"

"Well, what can a dude do about it?" growled Price. "You don't know? Well, let me tell ya! When your baby don't wantcha, you gotta do what ya gotta do. Know what that is?"

"N-o-o-o-o!!" echoed the crowd.

"You gotta get out the Jack. The Jack Daniels. When you and he become real familiar, you gotta, you gotta walk right up to your baby. That's right! You gotta walk right up to her and shout, "BA-BYYY, I WANNA JUMP YER BONES!"

There was absolute bedlam as 10,000 howling fans expressed their personal satisfaction. To compensate for the noise level, Price again adjusted the volume on his guitar. Cranking it up to ten, he danced into the spotlight that appeared once more center stage. Windmilling his right arm, he struck five impressive chords and then raised both fists over his head in a gesture of triumph. At that exact instant, a shower of sparks erupted from Vincent's instrument, and he jerked convulsively forward, toppling over his mic stand. As he wobbled to his knees, the audience was on its feet for a rousing ovation. It wasn't until the drummer had pounced from behind his kit to unplug

131

Price's amp that the crowd began to realize the guitarist's collapse wasn't part of the act.

Suddenly, the curtain tumbled down, and the stage was awash with roadies and security guards who gathered around Price as he writhed and contorted, near death. The head roadie even had the presence of mind to check Vincent's amplifier. When he noticed that the back was loose, he produced a screwdriver from his pocket and removed the cover. He was greeted by a horrible stench. Gagging, he backed away in search of reinforcements. He returned with a security guard in tow, and they spun the amp farther away from the stage wall to have a look inside. Their flashlight beams revealed the charred remains of a severed human hand lodged against a shorted transformer tube.

With the stench of bunt flesh strong in his nostrils, the head roadie remembered his conversation with Price before the show. On a hunch, he stumbled over to the towering bass cabinet and pried off the cover. The security guard had gone to vomit. Maybe it was just as well he didn't stick around, for the roadie was about to discover how a simple case of throat trouble had kept Willard from his light crew duties. What no one could explain was the vengeful leer that gleamed so horribly from the lyricist's decapitated head.

THE CRIMSON TINGE

Johnny pulled up in front of a purple mansion that sat sandwiched between two vacant brick homes. The painter did not shut off the motor right away but sat surveying the three-story dwelling with a professional eye and a foot poised over the gas pedal. He had heard all the wild rumors about the place and had a hard time disbelieving their validity as he studied the garish walls and barred windows. It didn't help matters that the rising sun shone directly on the painted house front, accenting its odd crimson tinge.

Johnny ran his hand across the two-day stubble sprouting on his face before turning off the ignition. A rumpled ball cap covered his unruly shock of snowy hair, and his soiled painter's clothes were dotted with faded splotches of tan and blue. "Shouldn'ta took this gol durn job," he grumbled as he climbed down from the patched seat of his pickup and hobbled around to yank open the sagging tailgate.

The truth of the matter was that Johnny hadn't worked all summer and was in no position to turn it down. He had botched several jobs the painters' union had set up for him earlier in the year, and they had pretty much written him off—until now. They had also conveniently failed to tell him that everyone else at the union hall had passed on this particular assignment after the first two painters had mysteriously disappeared from town. All that Johnny knew was that he had received a thousand dollars in advance just to finish part of the back wall!

Johnny hoisted a forty-foot ladder from the rack atop his pickup and weaved beneath its weight toward the spiked fence that surrounded the house. Fortunately, the gate had been left open, and he moved cautiously through it and then past six heavily curtained, barred windows around to the back of the house. The lawn felt spongy as cemetery grass beneath his feet.

With a grunt, the old man dropped the ladder and raised his eyes to study the back wall of the house. The other painters had scraped the entire surface with expert skill far beyond that now capable of his stringy muscles and creaking joints. They had even burned off some of the more stubborn chipped spots before priming and painting the back peak. Their work had stopped just above a curious, oval, stained glass window located two-thirds the way up the clapboard wall. Amber in hue, it was approximately five-feet wide and three-feet high. It was also the only window on that side of the house and the only one with no bars or curtains.

It took all the old man's strength to hoist the ladder into position well away from the window. "Get the gol durn thing eventually," he muttered while returning to his truck to retrieve a four-inch brush, two gallons of paint, and a drop cloth to spread on the ground beneath the ladder. Sure it was against standard procedure to do the lower part of the wall before finishing the window, but Johnny figured he might as well get the grunt work out of the way first.

Johnny knelt at the foot of the ladder and opened one of the unlabeled paint cans with his putty knife. Then, he withdrew a wooden stick from his coveralls and mixed the paint with a lifting motion. It took many minutes of patient stirring to blend in the queer, crimson swirl that had separated from the rest of the mixture and accounted for its abnormal hue. If this paint had not been sent with his thousand dollar check, Johnny knew he couldn't have matched it with any enamel he'd run across in forty years.

"Musta had the gol durn stuff imported," reasoned the old man as he examined the contents of the unlabeled can once more before starting up the ladder behind him. When he reached the top, he fished in his coveralls and produced an S-shaped hook that he employed to hang his paint pail from a convenient ladder rung. Then, he pulled a brush from another pocket and began applying the paint in long, smooth, practiced strokes. One coat covered the clapboards within his reach, and he climbed down to move the ladder closer to the window. He repeated the procedure twice more until he was two feet from the amber orb. At that point, he swung the ladder two feet to the other side of the window and continued across the side of the house. Afterward, he moved the ladder below the window to the next tier down. By so avoiding the fine trim work, he was able to finish the entire back wall by lunchtime.

Johnny returned to his pickup and snapped open a dented lunch pail. Since his wife died in '82, he had lived primarily on junk food. Today was no exception. As he wolfed down a bag of potato chips and a cold can of greasy spaghetti, he sat contemplating the crimson-tinged house with an unexplainable dread. There was just something about that color that gave even an unimaginative man like Johnny the creeps.

Shifting his gaze from the gaudy porch to the barred window above it, the painter saw the curtains part and then quickly close. With a shiver, he tossed the half-eaten can of spaghetti back into his lunch pail and rooted under the seat for a trim brush. He produced a paint-caked screwdriver, three pop bottles, and a moldy submarine sandwich before he finally located one.

"Time to get this dang place done and get outta here," growled Johnny when he returned to his workstation and stared up at the unpainted strip of clapboard surrounding the single window. "Gonna be a bitch, but I gotta do her!"

Johnny adjusted the ladder and raised it even with the top of the window. After restirring the paint, he climbed upward until he could reach the unpainted circle to the right of the amber orb. Then, he dipped his brush, wiped away the excess purple globs, and proceeded to "cut in" the stained glass pane. Although his hand shook with palsy, he used a skill gained through forty years of experience to deftly complete the task.

The old painter moved the ladder to the left of the window but did not scale it right away. Instead, he walked around on his toes to stretch his aching calf muscles. What he really needed was a quick nap, but somehow the thought of sleeping in the lengthening shadows of that odd-colored house wasn't exactly appealing. Also, the sky had become more overcast as the afternoon progressed, and the sun disappeared behind the clouds with alarming frequency. It was this observation that finally prodded Johnny back to work. One thing was for sure. He didn't want to get rained off and have to return tomorrow!

After Johnny reclimbed the ladder, the sun emerged from the clouds and reflected from the clapboards back into his eyes. Momentarily blinded, he squinted toward the window to get his bearings. It was at that exact instant the sun again dipped out of sight.

Johnny stared straight into the stained glass pane that was the replica of a human eye. Looking in through the pupil, he could distinctly see an attic loft of considerable dimension. Hanging upside down from the rafters of the vaulted ceiling were two human forms dressed in painter's coveralls. Tubes ran from each of the dangling arms into open paint cans on the floor.

Johnny grew faint and slumped forward against the ladder. As he did so, he dropped his bucket, spilling its contents down the side of the house. Clutching madly at the rungs above him, he managed to right himself. Before he fully regained his senses, he felt an added weight on the ladder below him. Somehow, he dared not look down. . .

THE GOLDENROD

Jacob Martin cut loose with a vile string of epitaphs as he struck out at a flight of bees that dive-bombed him from his blind side. It was swelteringly hot for the twenty-third of September, and the afternoon sun glinted from the row of red lumps that sprouted on the paunchy man's bald head. When he shifted the scythe from one sweaty paw to the other, the fresh bee stings made him wince with pain.

The fat man swore again. He was standing chest-deep in a sea of goldenrod that sprouted from the earth where his once bountiful garden had flourished. A continuous gaudy wave of weeds now stretched from the very steps of his porch to the distant hills aglow with crimson oaks. This was the third time in as many weeks that he had hewed a new path to his dog kennel located in the center of his backyard. The very thought of this annoyance threw Martin into another sudden fit of labor. With an anger oblivious to heat or pain, he hacked away at the arrow-straight stalks that hemmed him in. Ironically, the scythe was his only gardening tool that wasn't caked with rust.

A half hour later, an exhausted Jacob Martin chased off another swarm of attacking bees just as he reached the dog pen. With trembling fingers, he unlocked the gate and collapsed inside. He lay panting in the dirt until old Duke, his prize beagle, waddled from the kennel to lick his flushed cheeks. Jacob threw his arms around the hound and wheezed, "Thank God I made it to you, boy."

Outside the steel mesh enclosure, a shudder passed through the goldenrod. Saw-edged leaves wigwagged silent messages, and waving plumes of flower heads, heavy with insects, bent toward the pen as if in an attitude of listening. What resulted was the same faint rustling buzz that had kept the man tossing night after night in his bed. He recognized it instantly and huddled even closer to Duke. Strangely, there wasn't even a whisper of breeze.

Jacob could feel the sun burn through his tightly closed eyelids as he pondered with growing fear an enigma that had haunted him since spring. What still mystified him were the amazing regenerative powers of the goldenrod army that had invaded his property. He knew from research in the town library that the scientific name for the goldenrod was Solidago from the Latin "solidare," meaning to make whole. The plants were so-called because of their reputed curative powers. Until they had grown to five-foot in height in a week's time, he had always assumed that these curative powers referred to their potential benefit to the human species.

The only human to whom Jacob had dared confide this enigma was his neighbor, Aaron Shotts. Aaron was another gardening fanatic and had watched with alarm as the goldenrod spread in an almost calculated series of maneuvers from the foot of the distant hills to subjugate first his potato patch and then his prize-winning rose garden. Consequently, he had gladly joined forces with Jacob for a counterattack against the Solidago.

Jacob shook his head in wonderment while recalling the neighbors' attempt to annihilate their adversary. They had used a pesticide that he had never known to fail even on the most resilient strain of dandelion, and predictably the treated weeds shriveled and died. There was little time for celebration, though, for within two weeks a hardier army of goldenrod had sprung up to reclaim the garden plots. Upon its resurgence, the old men were shocked to learn that it now thrived upon the very pesticide that had previously choked it out. Some of the plants sprang up to six-foot in height. More shocking still, the bees also grew to gigantic proportions. The droning of these insects continued twenty-four hours a day as they feasted gluttonously upon their hosts.

Suddenly, Duke stiffened. The rustling of the goldenrod increased to a deafening level, but somehow the sound went undetected by the man huddled beside him. The hairs bristled on the hound's back, and he growled a low warning before disappearing tail-first into his kennel.

Despite his master's repeated coaxing, the dog remained cowering within.

Finally, Jacob staggered to his feet and stumbled from the protective walls of the dog pen. His heart fluttered uncertainly, and his head ached from his recent labor and the heat. When he found the path he had just blazed overgrown with even taller goldenrod, he began to question his own sanity.

Lunging forward in desperation, Jacob grabbed the nearest plants and attempted to uproot them with brute strength. He yelped and immediately withdrew his hands. Staring numbly at his left palm, he saw a jagged cut bisecting his lifeline.

The rustling of the saw-toothed leaves grew more violent still and blended with the buzzing of pollen-glutted insects. The sun glinted mockingly from the disk and ray florets. The earth began to spin beneath the man's feet as the gaudy plants towered over his head. Then, there was nothing but cool silence.

Aaron Shotts dozed fitfully at his writing desk and then woke with a start. Was that a scream or just his sodden brain playing tricks on him? Aaron leaned back in his chair to stretch his knotted shoulder muscles. Because he hadn't slept much in over a month, his face was now a mere caricature of its former self. His eyes were sunken and lusterless. His mouth drooped idiotically.

A faint rustle passed through the open window, and the old man glanced warily at the lengthening shadows spreading across his den. After noting the bloodred reflection of the late evening sun dancing on the wall, he mumbled, "I'd better go see how Jacob made out with his path-clearing project."

Aaron stamped woodenly across the yard that separated his split-level home from Jacob's identical residence. When a shudder passed through the sea of yellow flower heads bobbing in the backyard, he spotted a few single goldenrod stalks sprouting from his otherwise well-trimmed side yard. *Funny*, he thought, *those weren't there yesterday.* Quickening his pace, he made a mental note to return and uproot the pesky plants before they could choke out the grass between the houses, as well.

The lanky old man climbed onto his neighbor's front porch and rang the doorbell. An ominous buzz echoed briefly through the house. After several minutes' wait, Aaron rang it again. This time, the hum did not cease when he removed his finger from the button. Finally, he creaked open the door and called, "Jacob. Jacob? Are you—"

Aaron's voice strangled with terror when he found the living room transformed into a hive of buzzing insects. His eyes were drawn from the open window that admitted a steady stream of pollen-laden bees to the hexagonal patterns of honeycomb that encrusted the four walls and ceiling. It was then that he first heard the low, almost human howl emitting from the backyard.

Aaron backed down the porch steps without closing the door. Then, he bolted around the corner of the house and plunged neck-deep into the goldenrod jungle. As he thrashed toward the distant dog pen, the goldenrod stalks sprang to an even greater height in his wake. If his neighbor had cut a path earlier that afternoon, there was no evidence of it now.

The air was so heavy with pollen that Aaron's breathing came in rattling gasps by the time he had reached his objective. What he found just outside the steel mesh enclosure was enough to stifle his breathing altogether. There, beneath a swarm of feasting bees, lay Jacob Martin, his big bald head tilted back against the fence. It didn't take any coroner to tell he was dead. His vacant eyes stared skyward in the most ghastly fashion, and there was a hint of yellow powder around the corners of his mouth. The powder was the exact color of the flower heads that towered over the corpse. Conversely, the flesh of the dead man's face was the dull, bluish shade of a strangulation victim.

A shiver passed through Aaron as the sun set behind the distant oak-ridden hills. There was another sudden howl followed by a sharper rustling of the goldenrod.

THE EIGHTH WONDER OF THE WORLD

From an overlook built on a rocky hillside, Erik Johnson stared in awe at the Kinzua Viaduct that stretched from ridgetop to ridgetop 2,053 feet across the valley. The massive structure rose on twenty steel-plated legs from the murky gorge below. In clearer weather he would have seen that the center of the span was over three hundred feet tall. Even obscured by the July rain, to Johnson the viaduct still lived up to its billing as the Eighth Wonder of the World.

Watching the mist swirl about the black bridge, Erik said to his sister, who stood shivering beside him, "Hell of a day for Dad's funeral. I guess we better carry out his last request before another downpour drenches us."

"Yes, it seems weird coming here from such a solemn service," sighed Ruby, "especially after all the great times we had at this bridge picnicking with Grandma B."

"I just wish I'd been around in 1900 to see our great grandfather help rebuild the viaduct with steel. I always heard he was a fine Swedish craftsman. He also must have known a bit about having kids if you consider Grandma's ten siblings," chuckled Erik.

"How can you joke at a time like this?" snapped Ruby, tears welling in her blue eyes. "You're the one who's going to spread Dad's ashes over the Kinzua Valley."

"Then, let's get to it before I lose my nerve."

Erik left the overlook and led Ruby up a worn trail to the Kinzua Bridge State Park information area. He walked directly to the photos encased in glass. The images traced the history of the viaduct, and he was drawn to them every time he visited. These pictures were like old friends to him.

He was still amazed that a group of forty industrious men erected the prefabricated ironwork of the original bridge in just ninety-four days. That was in 1882 when all the workers had to aid them were two steam hoists, a gin pole, and a wooden crane. As he studied the crew's faces, Erik saw the same stubborn persistence that was ingrained in his own character.

"Are you going to stand there gawking all day?" whined Ruby, elbowing her brother in the ribs. "Come on. I'm cold."

"I'll bet you wouldn't be cold if you were looking for the gold buried out here," kidded Eric. "You know how many hours Uncle Dick has spent searching for it."

"Yeah. Yeah. I know all about the bank robber who hid his loot by a triangular rock within sight of the bridge. At least Dick's snooping allowed him to spot the rust that's been eating away at the support columns for years. I'm glad he told so many people. Without his lobbying, funds never would have been raised to begin the preservation work. Maybe we shouldn't go out there if Uncle Dick says the bridge is unsafe."

"No, it's all right. The state still hasn't closed it to foot traffic."

"I don't know. . .I'll bet if the repair crew guys weren't rained out today, they'd forbid us to walk over the gorge."

Erik turned up his collar as another squall sent a group of tourists scurrying for cover. A little rain couldn't drive him away after the times he had spent in the winter with his dad hunting whitetail deer that teemed near the bridge. Just up the valley, in the middle of a snowstorm, he had shot his first buck near Grant's Rocks. These rocks were named after President Ulysses S. Grant who came to McKean County to hunt with Kinzua Bridge founder, Thomas Kane, and killed a massive stag there. Although Erik's buck was only a four point, it signaled his passage into manhood and still ranked as one of his favorite memories.

"Erik, there you go daydreaming again," chided Ruby. "It looks like the weather's getting worse. I think we should leave."

"You always were the worrier of the Johnson clan," replied her brother. "We'll be okay."

"Even after hearing the severe weather advisory on the radio a thousand times while driving up here? I'm sorry, Erik. I'm going to wait in the car where it's safe."

"Okay, Sis. See you later."

As Ruby fought her way across the parking lot through the gusty wind, Erik's eyes misted over as he thought back to his many trips to the Kinzua Bridge with his father, Paul. They especially loved to come here to fly balsa wood airplanes they made from kits bought at Ruth Brothers' Hardware in Bradford. It took days to glue together the pieces and cover the wings and fuselages with tissue paper. After all that work, they glided their planes from the bridge toward Kushequa, knowing full well that they'd never recover them from the thick forest below. The gliders had rubber band powered engines and zoomed with the wind for miles until disappearing from sight.

"No wonder Dad wanted his ashes scattered over the Kinzua Valley," sighed Erik, as the treasured recollection drifted back into his subconscious.

Erik left the visitors' information stand and trudged toward the railroad tracks leading onto the Kinzua Viaduct. In his head he could hear his Uncle Dick's voice relating the history of the bridge:

"When General Thomas Kane returned from leading the Bucktail Regiment in the Civil War, he found his land in McKean County brimming with coal. With Buffalo, New York, using over three million tons of coal a year, Kane needed to find a way to carry his product to market. To accomplish this, he founded the New

147

York, Lake Erie, and Western Railroad and began laying track to the north. To get to Buffalo, he could either take a six mile detour around the Kinzua Valley or build this bridge. Kane decided to span the gorge when he learned how big a pile of greenbacks he would save. The general also wanted to overcome the challenge of building the world's highest bridge. He then contacted the brilliant engineer, Octave Chanute, who gave the bid to the Phoenixville Bridge Works. The rest, as they say, is history."

Johnson marched forward cradling his father's burial urn. He was unaware of the tears streaming down his face until a fierce wind smacked him as he proceeded onto the bridge walkway. The structure swayed and bucked beneath his feet until he found it increasingly difficult to maintain his balance. With a grim smile, Erik remembered the stories of such winds ripping the tops off boxcars and blowing whole cargoes of hemlock bark from the trains. That was why the engine speeds were regulated to five miles per hour when they chugged across the trestle.

As Erik inched along holding tightly to the railing, he recalled the time he and his dad were trapped here by a train. When the locomotive rumbled onto the viaduct, the swaying of the tracks intensified, causing Paul's face to turn white. With fearful eyes, the elder Johnson straddled a railing post and let his feet dangle in the air over the gorge below. He wedged Erik against the post and wrapped his powerful arms around him while the long string of coal cars jarred every bone in their bodies.

After the train rattled past, Paul stood and vomited over the railing. It wasn't until years later that Erik learned how his dad had nearly fallen from the roof of a roundhouse that serviced train engines in Bradford. Since his boyhood in the 1930's, Paul had successfully hidden his acrophobia until again faced with danger on the tallest bridge on the planet.

Erik fought he way across the viaduct until he could see the rain-swollen Kinzua Creek below him through the patchy mist. Gripping the urn in the crook of his arm, Johnson loosened the lid and said a final prayer for his father's soul. Afterward, he launched Paul's ashes into the wind and watched them blow violently off toward Kushequa.

The wind had now reached gale proportions, and it was all Erik could do to hang onto the railing. Fearfully, he stared across the valley at the leafy July woods that obscured the rocky terrain. It had been no problem for the builders to quarry sandstone blocks from the neighboring hills, he remembered. These were cut into stone piers and buried thirty-five feet into the ground to anchor the iron legs of the viaduct.

"Too bad the original anchor bolts weren't replaced when the bridge was rebuilt," muttered Erik, feeling the violent sway of the structure beneath him. "Those rusty bolts were the major concern that ended train traffic last year."

Johnson dropped to his knees and began crawling toward the park end of the bridge. It took every ounce of strength he could muster to fight the wind assailing him. The sky had turned the color of hard-boiled egg yolks and churned violently. When the wind swirled with tornado intensity, Erik clung desperately to the railing and watched the trees scalped from the hills. It was the last sight he remembered as the railing broke loose, hurling him into the abyss.

Erik extended his arms and legs and floated like a skydiver toward Grant's Rocks. The air was alive with singing shards of metal and splinters of wood. He closed his eyes to keep the wind from plucking them out and heard the bridge fight for its life behind him.

Erik glided along with the wind until he was rocked by a violent concussion that sent a sudden numbness through him. Opening his eyes, he found himself immersed in murky light. He felt someone grip his hand. He turned to find his father floating beside him, looking thirty-five again. Paul was dressed in his black and red hunting clothes. A broad grin stretched across his face as he pointed toward a glowing tunnel opening through the clouds ahead.

THE LONG WAY HOME

"Look out the window," said Mrs. Anderson with worry etched on her kind face. "The snow's really coming down. I think you should forget my painting and get home while you can."

Desmond Jones set down his paint pail next to the living room archway where he was working. Wiping his hands on his splattered bib overalls, he peered out at the fierce blizzard bombarding the neighborhood. Not only was the snow thick, but the wind whipped it sideways to create whiteout conditions.

"You're right, ma'am," replied Jones with a nervous smile. "First, I'll pick up my drop cloths."

"No, you just go ahead, Dessie. I'll straighten up. You have dangerous hills to travel."

"Thanks, Mrs. Anderson. I'll clean my brush and be on my way. I'll bet school lets out early this afternoon. I'd like to get out of town before the slick roads are clogged with all that bus traffic."

Desmond strode to the kitchen sink and ran warm water on his two-inch cut brush. Staring out at the raging squall, it seemed to take forever to rinse the white paint from the bristles. White always stayed in the brush longer, anyway, and Jones had to bite his tongue to keep from cussing. He surely didn't want to offend this nice lady who had hired him in the middle of a tough winter. To stem his impatience, he hummed a Jimmy Buffett tune until the job was complete.

Returning to the living room, he found Mrs. Anderson holding his coat and tool box. "Have a safe trip," she said. "Call me when you get home, so I won't worry."

"Yes, ma'am. Thanks for everything."

When Desmond opened the front door, a gust of wind nearly bowled him over. The Anderson home was built on a side hill, and he skated down a slick set of steps to snow-covered Belleview Avenue below. There was already a foot of heavy slop on the ground and no sign of it letting up.

The painter yanked on his gloves, brushed off the door of his Ford Taurus, and inserted his key in the lock. The lock was frozen and wouldn't budge, so he hustled around to the passenger side. He vigorously tried this lock until it finally clicked. The door itself, however, was encased with ice. He reefed on the handle with all his might before the door swung outward with a grating creak.

Fetching his scraper from the dashboard, Jones scurried about like a monkey as he cleaned off the windshield. The snow was coming down so hard that he barely completed the task when he was forced to start over twice more. Finally, in disgust, he leaped behind the steering wheel, fired up the engine, and turned the windshield wipers on "high" to clear his vision for the hazardous drive home.

Desmond eased his Taurus into gear and crept along Belleview Avenue. The street was unplowed, and he could only manage five miles an hour without skidding toward the row of parked vehicles lining the curb. Belleview wound parallel with the hill and then made a sharp right turn to plummet to the street below. When Jones tried to negotiate this curve, he slid dangerously toward a ditch that ran between the road and the last house on Belleview. Pumping his brakes, he stopped just before his car careened into the snowy trench.

Sweat soaked his face as Desmond backed his vehicle onto the flat lane above the curve. Carefully cutting his wheels, he started forward at two miles an hour and again skated toward the ditch. Wildly, he spiked the brakes, only stopping inches from disaster. After backing up a second time, he then rolled down the hill at one mile an hour. The street had become even greasier from his spinning wheels, and his Taurus slid almost sideways before he got it under control.

With frustration glittering in his eyes, Desmond jerked his auto in reverse and spun up the hill for another try. His stomach churned, and his hands trembled on the wheel. Several cars were behind him now, too, waiting to exit Belleview. In his side mirror he could see the lips of the impatient drivers dissecting his incompetence. No one was going to move until he did, so he put aside his anxiety and once more eked his Taurus into low gear.

Jones kept way to the left on this descent and finally steered clear of trouble. Keeping his foot on the brake, he inched down the steep hill toward Jackson Avenue where a steady stream of school buses rolled past. He didn't dare go any faster, or he'd skid into the flow of traffic and cause a horrific accident.

It took Desmond ten minutes to go a hundred yards. When he finally reached the foot of the hill, his body shook, and a vague headache throbbed in his temples. Luck was finally with him, though, for a bus stopped up the block, and children spewed out its folding door. This allowed Jones to pull directly onto Jackson Avenue and head for home.

Although Jackson was a main artery through Bradford, it, too, was extremely slick from the steady, falling snow. "Dang!" muttered Desmond as he crept along. "If it's this slippery in town, what's Red Rock Hill going to be like? Any other day, I'd be back in Duke Center by now."

The painter continued to go no faster than ten miles an hour down the busy rush hour street. He pumped his brakes well before each stop sign because he knew from years of winter driving that stopping and starting vehicles turned intersections into skating rinks. By using extreme caution, he was able to reach Bolivar Drive without incident. There, the traffic thinned, so Desmond speeded up to fifteen and proceeded into the country.

The weather became more severe with each mile Jones drove. When he finally reached the little village of Derrick City, he could barely see twenty yards ahead of him. Drifts were now piling up on the road, making the going even tougher. Each time he hit one, it reminded him of riding his fishing boat through rough waves. Wiping the steam off the windshield, he peered anxiously ahead. Everywhere, snow coated the trees, obscuring the most prominent landmarks. To the painter, even the oil jacks looked cold.

I shouldn't have come out today, Desmond thought as he plowed through the deepening ruts. *But how could I disappoint a customer who feeds me lunch every day and treats me like a son? I have a reputation for reliability, too. If I had a dollar for every time the weatherman was wrong, I could retire to the Florida Keys.*

Desmond kept a slow, steady pace until he came to the junction of Derrick and Rock City Roads. There, a squad car with flashing, red lights blocked the highway. A shivering officer dressed in a uniform jacket and a pointed hat signaled for him to stop and turn around.

"So is Red Rock Hill closed?" asked Jones after cranking down his side window.

"No, I'm auditioning for the Eskimo Club," growled the freezing policeman. "Why else would I be out here?"

"Are any of the roads to Duke Center open?"

"What do you think, Buster? Look at this crap come down!"

Instead of responding with a snappy comeback, Desmond punched the gas. Blasting slop from his churning wheels, he spun his vehicle in a circle and fishtailed back the way he had come. Glancing in the side mirror, he could see the splattered policeman shaking his fist at him. Jones chuckled with satisfaction and then muttered, "That'll teach the SOB! Maybe he'll be nicer to the next guy who asks him a simple question."

As Desmond pushed forward toward Bradford, a worried frown crossed his thin face. "What should I do now?" he wondered aloud. "With all the hills closed, I'll never get home. Unless. . ."

Jones increased his speed to twenty miles an hour and bucked his sturdy Ford through the last snow-clogged miles to Route 219. There, he crept up the on ramp and merged with a stream of passenger cars and big rigs headed due north. After he settled into line, he said with a grin, "Why didn't I think of this before? All I gotta do is take the long way home through Olean, Portville, and Eldred. It's flat the whole way. If I take it easy, I'll be in DC well before dark."

Desmond's smile suddenly evaporated when a semi closed hard on his back bumper and began blowing a series of strident horn blasts. The highway was so slick that he had again slowed to fifteen, much to the trucker's annoyance. Jones was hemmed in on the left by an oil tanker, too, and the sweat stood out on his brow as the two trucks squeezed him.

Finally, the tanker inched past, and the other semi whipped out into the passing lane with its trailer weaving dangerously behind it. Dessie slowed even further and crowded the slushy berm to keep from being sideswiped. The trailer missed his Taurus by inches as it swayed by. The trucker naturally issued another salvo from his air horn.

When Jones reached the Cow Palace exit, he took it. Tears streamed from his eyes, and his nerves were frayed to the limit. As he again headed back to Bradford, he croaked, "Only one chance left. G-g-guess I'll try Looker Mountain."

The road crews were hard at work in the city when Desmond arrived there. The sand trucks sent orbs of yellow light spiraling from their rooftops as they spread their gift along the streets. This settled the painter down. He turned with renewed hope onto South Kendall Avenue and started toward home through a steady curtain of sleet.

The sleet now presented a new challenge that Dessie's windshield wipers couldn't handle. Soon, he was forced to pull off the road and knock the ice from the rubber wiper blades so he could see to drive. He only managed another mile before he stopped to repeat the process. Luckily, he drove out of the nasty precipitation just as he reached the turnoff for Looker Mountain Trail.

This road was a total mess as the wind drifted snow and created whiteout conditions. All Desmond could do was keep his car between the guardrails and forge on. To quell his apprehension, he mumbled, "Man, am I glad they invented front wheel drive. If I had the old Maverick, I'd be rotta ruck. Don't know how many time I spun sideways up over the hill in that heap. That was when I worked second shift at Case Cutlery, and poor Betty Kervin rode back and forth with me. She got so nervous when we'd start to skid, she broke into fervent prayer."

Jones chuckled at the memory and then stared through his fogged windshield at the long straightaway leading to the foot of the mountain ahead. Snow plastered the trees on either side of the road, making a grim tunnel through which to roll. Gunning his engine, he accelerated to forty miles an hour to begin his ascent up the long, gradual slope. He had his gas pedal jammed to the floor and only let up on it if he started to slide.

"Got a good run for the hill!" he cackled. "Just hope my speed holds."

Desmond continued to make decent progress until he reached the right curve halfway up the mountain. Here, he churned past numerous wrecked vehicles slammed up against the guardrails. Many of the cars were so smashed that it looked as though they'd been rammed. Yet, there were no multi-car pileups that would cause such damage. Even more curious, he passed no drivers looking for help.

With his hands in a death grip on the wheel, Desmond reached the last steep incline leading to the top of the mountain. Yelping "Bonsai," he again tromped on the gas and surged forward as his tires churned and smoked and sprayed snow. His vehicle climbed with urgency now because a silver SUV was blasting along just behind him for all it was worth.

When Jones' Taurus finally spun to the summit, the four-by-four on his tail shot past him and careened down the Rixford side of the mountain. "What got into that crazy fool?" Dessie grunted as his windshield again iced over, this time on the inside. "Hey, where'd the road go? Hey!"

Before Desmond could grab his scraper from the dashboard, he found himself sliding out of control on the icy, downhill slope. Pumping his brakes only worsened the problem, so he downshifted into low. Out of instinct he hit the brakes when he continued to skid. This caused him to spin in a complete circle and slam backward into a ditch. Shrieking with terror, he ripped open his door and scrambled from behind the wheel. After wiping blood from a cut on his cheek, he stared wide-eyed at his wrecked car. It looked like the ditch had eaten his Taurus by the way it protruded from the yawning hole in the snow.

Jones turned up his coat collar and stomped dejectedly back to the ridgetop. He panted with fatigue and felt sick inside. Soon, he heard an engine laboring up Looker Mountain Trail, so he turned to stare down its treacherous slope. He didn't wait long before a yellow PennDOT sand truck came chugging up the hill toward him. Desmond's chapped lips cracked into a relieved smile, and he waved and shouted to attract the driver's attention. As the vehicle rumbled nearer, Dessie saw that its blade wasn't down. No sand was spewing from the back, either.

"Is that fellow drunk, or what?" raged the painter to the gusting wind. "Is—"

Jones' other question stuck in his throat when he spotted a mane of white, shaggy hair in the oncoming cab. Clawed fingers clutched the wheel, and glowing, yellow eyes glowered at him hungrily through the shattered glass where a human head had smashed the windshield. He then knew why there were so many battered vehicles littering the hill and why the SUV passed him on the summit at maniacal speed.

"It's the Abominable Snowman driving that truck!" screamed Desmond. "The Abominable freaking Snowman!"

ABOUT THE AUTHOR

William P. Robertson was born in Bradford, Pennsylvania in 1950. After graduating with honors from Mansfield University in 1972, he began writing horror as a release from Sunlight Deprivation Syndrome that plagues him each winter. He soon created his own brand of Gothic terror that has been published in magazines worldwide. In his spare time, Bill enjoys fishing for trout, following the Pittsburgh Pirates, and taking spooky photos of the desolate region where he lives. According to Robertson, "It was my Swedish grandmother Bernadine who first got me interested in ghosts and trolls. She was a great storyteller!" To learn more about the author's work, visit **http://www.thehorrorhaven.com.**

BOOKS BY WILLIAM P. ROBERTSON

Short Story Collections

Lurking in Pennsylvania (2004), *Dark Haunted Day* (2006), *Terror Time* (2009), *The Dead of Winter* (2010), *Season of Doom* (2013), *Terror Time 2nd Edition* (2013), *Stories from the Olden Days* (2015), *Misdeeds and Misadventures* (2016), *More Stories from the Olden Days* (2017), *Love That Burns* (2017), *War in the Colonies* (2018).

Novels

Hayfoot, Strawfoot: The Bucktail Recruits (2002), *The Bucktails' Shenandoah March* (2002), *The Bucktails: Perils on the Peninsula* (2006), *The Bucktails' Antietam Trials* (2006), *The Battling Bucktails at Fredericksburg* (2006), *The Bucktails at the Devil's Den* (2007), *The Bucktails' Last Call* (2007), *Ambush in the Alleghenies* (2008), *Attack* in the Alleghenies (2010), *This Enchanted Land: The Saga of Dane Wulfdin* (2010), *The Bucktail Brothers of the Fighting 149th* (2011), *The Bucktail Brothers: Brave Men's Blood* (2012), *The 190th Bucktails: Catchin' Bobby Lee* (2014), *Annihilated in the Alleghenies* (2016).

Poetry Volumes

Burial Grounds (1977), *Gardez Au Froid* (1979), *Animal Comforts* (1981), *Life After Sex Life* (1983), *Waters Boil Bloody* (1990), *1066* (1992), *Hearse Verse* (1994), *The Illustrated Book of Ancient, Medieval & Fantasy Battle* Verse (1996), *Desolate Landscapes* (1997), *Bone Marrow Drive* (1997), *Ghosts of a Broken Heart* (2005), *Icicles* (2018), *Lost* (2018).

Audio Books

Gasp! (1999), *Until Death Do Impart* (2002), *Bucktail Tales* (2013).